I0827434

MISSING PIECES

Reese Wordlaw

Book Cover Design: Reese Wordlaw

First edition

Dedication

I dedicate this work to my Heavenly Father for blessing me with the ability to co-create with Him..

To my children - Angel, Charity, Faith, and Ira III - who taught me the meaning of true love.

To my grandchildren, London and Karter - the future I can rest in and love without measure.

My love for you all is eternal.

To my parents - for the love you give and life you gave – thank you.

To my sisters, I love you.

To my greatest friend and sister - Bradlie Elverton, and my goddaughter, Cierra Taylor - your encouragement carries me more than you know. I love you both beyond words.

Reese

Prologue

I don't remember the exact moment everything inside me shattered.

There wasn't a single event I could isolate and say, *that's where it happened.* No clean break or loud collapse.

It was quieter. Loss layered over loss. Disappointments repeating until it stopped surprising me.
Circumstances stacking until something stuck.

What stuck…stayed.

And what stayed became a rule.

Stay detached. Don't get too close.

It wasn't a decision. It was an imperceptible pattern formed through repetition. Through watching what disappeared the moment you depended on it over and over again.

When life changed, I adapted.

That's what men do. We assess. Adjust our footing. Shift the weight. Keep what's stable, discard what isn't. Even when what no longer holds once mattered.

I learned how to stay useful. How to succeed without settling.
How to connect without attaching.
And how to give just enough to be respected, just enough to be wanted, just enough to position myself to be missed.

From the outside, it looked like strength.
Like discipline.
Like a man with direction.

From the inside, it felt safe.
Everything calculated, contained and controlled. Nothing left unattended long enough to grow roots.

I was good at arranging my life so nothing ever asked too much of me.

I told myself this was wisdom.
Maturity.
Manhood.

And for a while, it worked.

But if you stood too close to me in those years, if you lingered in the places I hadn't learned how to soften - you would feel it.

Not anger. Not cruelty. Distance.

That slow burn of yearning for more that scorches over time.

I wasn't reckless but I became very deliberate.

Deliberate with my words, with my time and what parts of myself I allowed to surface.

And somewhere along the way, without ceremony or warning, I became a man who could assemble everything around him with precision…but myself.

The Broken Frame

The thunder came before the storm.

It wasn't raining yet, but the sky over the neighborhood had turned the color of purplish grey, heavy and waiting. Streetlights flicked on earlier than they should have, halos of dull yellow in the growing gray. I sat at the dining room table with a thousand tiny cardboard pieces scattered in front of me, trying to build something complete while the house slowly fell apart.

My mother said this puzzle was "grown-up."

A city skyline at night. Dark buildings stacked against a navy sky, lights reflected on a strip of black water. The pieces were smaller - a thousand of them.

"You're double digits now," she'd said. "Ten deserves more of a challenge."

I liked hearing that.

I liked the way each piece felt between my fingers - cool, a little rough at the edges, precise. I liked turning them over and letting the mess slowly make sense. Corners first, then the edges. That was the rule. Once you frame it, the middle knows where to go.

That was what my father taught me.

Upstairs, voices pressed through the ceiling.

They weren't shouting. Not exactly. But they'd moved past the quiet, careful tone adults use when they think kids aren't listening. This was that in-between kind of arguing. Low. Controlled. Heavy. The kind that made the walls feel thinner.

I picked up a corner piece that was more shadow than sky and fit it against the bottom edge. It clicked into place. A small sound. A small victory.

I focused on the puzzle on purpose. My world was spread out on that table, blue and black and tiny colored squares pretending to be windows. If I concentrated hard enough, I could almost mute the words I couldn't quite hear above.

Almost.

A drawer slammed somewhere upstairs. Then a sharp crack of something hitting a wall. My mother's voice shot through the ceiling, rising, cracking on its way down.

"Are you're leaving us for her?"

The word "her" landed first.

Then "us."

My hand stilled over the pile of pieces. The room felt like it inhaled and held its breath.

My father answered, but I couldn't hear the words. Only the tone. Measured. Like he had already decided how much of himself he was willing to give to this moment.

"You're not even trying anymore," my mother said.

Silence followed.

Heavy.

Not empty—full.

Then -

"It's his birthday, Howard."

That part came through clean.

Like it was meant to.

I stared at the puzzle box.

Thunder rolled in the distance as if the sky was answering for me.

I stared at the puzzle box. The picture on the lid looked neat, easy, obvious. Everything in its place. No empty spaces. No missing pieces.

I looked down at the table. Corners done. Bottom edge halfway built. Top edge untouched. The middle a wild mess of confusion and scattered pieces.

Footsteps moved on the stairs. Slower than usual.

My mother came into the dining room, wiping at her face quickly like she'd just splashed water on it. Her hair was pulled into a loose bun that had slipped a little, and her apron was on backward. She stopped when she saw me at the table and forced a smile that didn't quite fit.

"Hey, birthday boy," she said, voice softer than her eyes. "You are serious about that thing, huh?"

I nodded, fingers still on the pieces. "Almost done with the bottom."

"Mm." She walked past me to the kitchen counter where the cake sat waiting, chocolate frosting smoothed as perfectly as she could manage earlier when the day still held promise. "Looks good."

I watched her pull out the box of candles. Ten white sticks. She set them down but didn't open them yet. Her hands hovered for a second like she couldn't remember what came next.

She sat and chat with me, helped me place a few pieces.

About an hour later, we heard footsteps on the stairs behind us.

I turned my head.

My father was coming down, two duffel bags hanging from his shoulders.

Not the slim work bag he carried every day.

They were bigger. Softer. The kind people use when they intend to stay somewhere else awhile.

He moved quietly, like he didn't want to disturb something that was already fragile.

"Hey," he said.

The word went mostly to the room, but landed near me.

"Hey," I answered, because not saying it would have hurt more.

My mother didn't turn around. "You're late," she said. Her voice sounded tired, no edges now. Just worn. "It's his birthday."

My father's jaw worked once. "I'm here, ain't I?"

He set the duffels near the bottom of the stairs with a quiet hesitation like he wasn't sure whether to hold or put them down. It was long enough to say what he hadn't yet said out loud. Mom and I watched and for a moment, no one moved.

Then his eyes dropped to the table. To the chaos of blue pieces, the half-built frame, the box with its perfect printed version of what the mess could become.

"You're doing it like I taught you," he said, and there was the faintest flicker of pride in his tone. "Outer frame first."

I met his eyes.

He stepped closer, nodding toward the pieces. "Once the edges are set, the middle makes sense."

It sounded like something he might say on any other day, like we were just two people talking about puzzles. But something felt off. The words hit wrong with that duffel sitting by the stairs.

"How do you know where everything goes?" I heard myself ask.

He paused. It was a small pause, but I caught it. The kind of pause where honesty tries to decide whether it should show up or stay quiet.

"You don't," he said finally. "You just… do what you can."

He said it like it was wisdom. Like it explained the bag. The storm. The shaking in my mother's hands.

He picked up the duffels again.

"Dad, can you help me with this part." I said quickly, pointing down toward the mid-section of the puzzle.

"I'll come by tomorrow," he told me. "We'll do it then. Just us."

The words floated between us. Light but heavy.

I nodded because that's what sons do. "Okay."

He'd never lied to me, but I felt uncertainty in his voice.

My mother turned then, gripping the edge of the counter behind her as if it were all that kept her standing.

"Say what you came to say, Howard."

My father's gaze flicked to her, then dropped. "I already did."

He shifted the strap on his shoulder. "Be good for your mom," he said to me.

Then he turned and went back up the stairs, the duffel bumping softly against his leg with each step.

The thunder finally broke.

Rain came down heavy, and the house felt quieter in its wake.

My mother stared at the space where he'd been, her chest rising and falling once, twice, like she was reminding herself to breathe. Then she blinked hard and reached for the cake knife.

"We'll do the cake tomorrow," she said, not looking at me.

I swallowed. The piece in my fingers had gone warm from my grip.

"It won't be my birthday tomorrow," I said.

She froze, just for a second. Her head bowed slightly like the weight of that truth was too much.

"I know," she murmured.

The clock on the wall ticked three times.

Somewhere in the house, the air conditioner kicked on.

I looked back at the puzzle. One piece sat near the top where the sky should close. It wasn't the right one. The shape was off. The color a little too dark. But my hand moved almost on its own, lifting it, turning it, trying to make it fit anyway.

I pressed it into the wrong gap and held it there. It didn't click. It just sat, crooked and forced.

For a moment, I left it like that.

Then I let go.

The piece slid away from the edge and fell back into the scatter with the others.

I didn't try to fix it.

I just sat there.

Looking at something that was supposed to come together

and realizing it may never again.

My mother moved the cake to the fridge. The candles stayed in the box.

I felt paralyzed, my body couldn't move. I kept staring at the incomplete frame, until the edges blurred and the colors ran together.

My chest felt tight, but the tears stopped somewhere before my eyes. They settled deeper, in a place I didn't have words for.

That night, I didn't throw the puzzle or sweep it to the floor. I didn't destroy the picture.

I just didn't add another piece.

When I finally pushed back from the table and turned off the dining room light, the skyline on the box still looked perfect. Complete. Whole.

The one on the table would never reach perfection.

I went to bed knowing one thing for sure.

My father had left.

I wouldn't realize until much later that something else had left with him.

The puzzle stayed unfinished downstairs.

And so did the boy who started it.

Silent Answers

The first call happened the morning after my father left.

I waited until the sun pushed a thin line of gold across my bedroom carpet. I sat up slowly, carrying the heaviness that comes after a night where sleep isn't really sleep - just waiting for morning to arrive.

For a few seconds, I lay still and listened.

Sometimes when I was little, if I waited long enough, I could hear my father moving around downstairs before I got up. The clink of his coffee mug. The sound of the front door opening too early. His footsteps on the porch.

That morning, there was only quiet.

The house felt like it was holding its breath.

My mother was already awake. I could hear faint kitchen sounds, the familiar rhythm of bowls and spoons. She'd always been an early riser, but that morning the quiet felt different. Thicker. Like the walls themselves were bracing.

I stared at the phone on my nightstand.

It looked bigger somehow. Heavier. Like the act of calling would take more strength than I had.

Still, I picked it up and dialed the number I could do in the dark.

Ring.
Ring.
Ring.

Voicemail.

This is Howard. Leave a message.

For a moment, I almost smiled.

Hearing his voice felt close enough to comfort.

I waited, half-expecting him to interrupt his own voicemail. To answer late. To say my name.

He didn't.

I exhaled slowly.

I didn't leave a message.

Not because I didn't have anything to say.

But because I didn't know how to make my voice sound normal if I spoke.

Maybe he was with a client.
Maybe he didn't hear it.
Maybe his phone was in the other room.

Maybe he'd call back first, the way fathers should.

I held onto that thought longer than I probably should have.

I set the phone down and got dressed.

Downstairs, my mother was stirring oatmeal like she was trying to keep her own hands busy. Her back was turned when I walked in. She didn't turn around. She didn't say anything about the cake in the fridge or the unopened candles on the counter.

It wasn't denial.

It was exhaustion.

"Morning," I said, sliding into my usual chair.

"Morning," she replied, her voice soft but steady. "Eat before it gets cold."

I nodded.

Neither of us mentioned the empty chair.

Neither of us looked at it.

After breakfast, I went outside and shot hoops in the driveway. The ball thudded against the concrete and bounced back to me. Over and over. The rhythm felt grounding. Predictable. Something I could count on.

I made myself believe that if I kept doing normal things, normal would come back.

At one point I stopped and looked up at the sky. It was clear now — washed clean by the storm. The kind of blue that looked like it should belong to a good day.

For a second, I felt almost okay.

That scared me.

Before lunch, I tried calling again.

Ring.
Ring.
Ring.

Voicemail.

I hung up before the beep.

By midweek, calling became its own ritual.

A quiet one.
A hopeful one.
A necessary one.

I didn't announce it.
I didn't check the time.
Sometimes I dialed before I even realized I'd reached for the phone.

Always the same ring.
Always the same greeting.
Always the same silence after.

Each time I waited just a little longer before hanging up.

Each time I told myself it didn't mean anything.

I tried to imagine what he was doing.

Was he sitting somewhere by a window?
Driving?
Laughing?
Sleeping in?
Listening to another woman ask questions that used to belong to my mother?

It was astonishing how fast an adult could rearrange a life while a child was still sweeping up the pieces.

One afternoon my mother asked if I wanted to go to the grocery store with her.

I shook my head. "I'll start my homework."

She studied me for half a second, like she felt the shift but didn't know where to place it.

"Alright," she said softly.

When she left, I picked up the phone again.

Voicemail.
Voicemail.
Voicemail.

I pressed the receiver to my ear until the disconnected tone buzzed against my skin.

I told myself I just wanted to hear his voice again.

I didn't cry.

I didn't throw the phone.

I didn't even tell my mother.

I just set the receiver down gently, like it might break if I wasn't careful.

At school, nothing changed and everything changed.

I answered my teachers with the same yes ma'am, no sir.
I sat at lunch with the same kids.
I played the same games at recess.

But I listened differently.

Every loud voice made me turn my head.

Every adult man passing the fence made me look twice.

I didn't realize I was searching until I noticed I was always disappointed.

My homeroom teacher asked about my birthday.

"How was the cake?" she smiled.

"It was good," I said.

That was the first time I realized I could tell a lie without thinking.

I wasn't protecting my father.

I was protecting myself from explaining something I didn't understand yet.

I walked home slower that day.

Not to avoid the house —
but to delay stepping into its quiet.

The puzzle stayed on the table the first few days.

My mother worked around it carefully.

She dusted without touching it.
Wiped the table without wiping under it.
Moved bowls and magazines around it.

It sat there like a promise that hadn't decided what it was yet.

On the fourth morning, I came downstairs and the space was clean.

The puzzle was gone.

My mother was tying up a trash bag, pulling the knot tight.

There was a long pause between us.

"There wasn't any point leaving it half-done," she said without turning around.

I wanted to say something.

I wanted to ask if she'd finished it.

I wanted to ask if she'd thrown it away.

I wanted to ask if things ever come back once they leave.

I said nothing.

I just nodded.

She didn't see it.

I went outside and sat on the porch steps for a long time. The air was cool, crisp in a way that made the world feel taller. Trees rustled overhead, leaves whispering secrets to each other.

And something settled into me - not anger, not sadness, but a kind of quiet understanding:

My father had always stopped in the middle.

Conversations.
Promises.
Birthdays.
Life.

I had learned how to wait for what never came.

And waiting taught me to expect empty spaces.

That night, lying in bed, the hum of the refrigerator downstairs comforted me.

Not because it sounded like someone was moving.

But because it stayed.

When I finally closed my eyes, I didn't dream.

I didn't toss.

I didn't cry.

I rested inside a silence that felt new.

Not empty.

Just… different.

Not all losses are loud.

Some arrive softly, carrying hope with them at first, until hope learns how to sit beside disappointment without breaking.

Still Waiting

I didn't stop hoping all at once.

Hope didn't leave in a dramatic way. It didn't slam a door or make an announcement. It just grew quieter, like it learned it wasn't welcome to speak out loud anymore.

It learned how to sit in the background while I did my homework at the kitchen table, pencil tapping softly against paper. While I shot baskets alone in the driveway, counting my own rebounds. While I ate dinner at a table with one empty chair no one mentioned, like silence could make it disappear.

Hope learned how to fold itself into ordinary days and not ask for too much attention.

But it stayed.

It stayed in the way I still listened for the sound of a car pulling into the driveway at night, even after I knew better. In the way my heart jumped just a little whenever headlights passed the house. In the way I noticed every man who walked with his shoulders a certain way and wondered, for just a second, if it was him.

My father was not a villain in my memory.

He was the man who lifted me onto the kitchen counter so I could reach the cereal, steadying me with one hand on my back. The one who showed me how to skip stones across the water and how to hold a basketball so it spun right off my fingers. He smelled like clean soap and something woody I couldn't name. He laughed loudly at his own jokes and always insisted on controlling the radio on long drives, even when everyone else complained.

He wasn't gentle exactly.

But he was present.

He wasn't soft.

But he was familiar. Practical. Solid in a way I didn't yet have words for.

He was the voice that said my name in a way that made me feel chosen. The one who called me "buddy" like it meant something important. The one who believed that fixing things with your hands was the same as fixing things in life.

When he left, he didn't just take love with him.

He took continuity.

He took the shape my days had learned how to hold.

He took the person I looked to who knew how life was supposed to go.

When I imagined him walking back in, I didn't imagine apologies. I imagined him standing in the doorway with that crooked half-smile, like he wasn't sure he was welcome but hoped he was. I imagined him saying my name first. Not my mother's. Mine.

I imagined that because that was how he used to arrive in my life. Every day.

And every day he didn't walk through that front door became a disappointment that felt like gravity. A gentle, constant pull that taught me how to lower my expectations just enough that they wouldn't hurt when they landed.

It taught me how to brace myself quietly.

How to want things without needing them.

How to keep parts of myself untouched so they couldn't be taken from me.

I didn't know I was learning these things.

I only knew the world felt different now. That something had shifted, and I was shifting with it, the way a house settles when the ground beneath it changes.

I started noticing patterns.

How people left conversations early. How promises were often shaped like hope but built like smoke. How adults said things they didn't always mean and meant things they didn't always say. I began to listen not for what people spoke, but for what they avoided.

I began to trust what was consistent instead of what was passionate.

The mailman came every afternoon.
The neighbor's dog barked every morning.
The sun slid through the kitchen window at the same angle near dinnertime.

Those things became reliable.

People did not.

That wasn't bitterness.

It was observation.

I learned how to anchor myself to what stayed.

At school, I still raised my hand.
Still got good grades.

Still laughed at jokes that weren't that funny.
Still ran fast and jumped high and tried hard.

From the outside, I looked like a boy doing just fine.

From the inside, I felt like a boy holding something fragile he didn't quite understand.

Sometimes I wondered if other boys carried things like this too. If their chests tightened for no visible reason. If they ever woke up missing someone before they even knew who it was. If they ever felt older than their age and younger than their longing at the same time.

But boys didn't talk about that.

So I didn't either.

I carried it quietly.
Into my teenage years.
Into my friendships.
Into the way I listened.
Into the way I loved things just enough, but not too much.

Just close enough.
But not all the way.

I didn't know yet that this was becoming a shape.
A way of being.
A way of surviving.

That night, lying in bed, I listened to the steady hum of the refrigerator downstairs. It had become something like comfort since he left. Not because it sounded like someone was there, but because I could trust it to stay.

I let my eyes close to that sound. Let my breathing fall into its rhythm. Let myself rest on something that didn't promise more than it could give.

I guess I felt safe.

And for a boy who had just learned that some things could disappear without warning, that was enough to fall asleep.

I didn't know then that this moment would become a template. That I would spend years trying to recreate this feeling of quiet steadiness. That I would search for it in work, in achievement, in connection, in motion.

That I would confuse calm with safety.
And safety with love.
That I would mistake consistency for intimacy.
And distance for strength.

I didn't know that yet.

All I knew was that something in me had changed.
Not broken.
Changed.

Like water finding a new path through dry, cracked ground.

Quiet Shifts

Time didn't stop after my father left.

It just changed speed.

Some days moved in slow motion, every hour stretching like gum. Other days jumped forward in uneven skips, morning and then suddenly evening, with the middle blurred by routine. There were no big announcements, no dramatic breakdowns, no slammed doors after that night. Just small adjustments.

My father's coffee mug disappeared from the dish rack.

His work shoes vanished from their spot by the door.

The scent of his cologne, once trapped in the hallway like a ghost, faded day by day until I had to close my eyes and try to remember it.

My mother changed, but not in the way movies showed women falling apart. She got up. Went to work. Paid bills. Folded laundry. Asked about my homework. She moved like someone who had decided that stopping was not an option.

But there were other changes too.

Smaller ones.

Quieter ones.

She sat down more often.

She rubbed her temples like they hurt.

Sometimes she paused halfway up the stairs, just for a second, like she was catching her breath.

The only giveaway was how she moved in the mornings.

She used to hum when she cooked. Old church songs, bits of R&B from the radio, whatever had stuck in her head. Sometimes she'd dance a little while flipping pancakes, just a shoulder roll or hip sway, making the kitchen feel warmer than it was.

Now the kitchen was quiet.

Not cold. Just deliberate. Every sound was practical. Pan. Spoon. Cabinet. Water.

No humming.

I noticed.

But I said nothing.

Ten year old boys don't ask their mothers why the music stopped.

I noticed how she held the counter when she stood too long.

How she leaned her hip against the sink when she washed dishes.

How she sometimes pressed her hand to her chest like she was steadying something inside herself.

I didn't know what it meant.

I only knew it was different.

So I adjusted too.

After school I dropped my backpack in my room, changed uniforms for overworn play clothes, and either went to shoot hoops out front or sat on the couch and watched whatever was on TV. My shows didn't feel as funny as before, but laughing out loud felt like a betrayal, so mostly I watched in silence.

At night I did homework at the dining table while my mother washed dishes in the kitchen. The bare space where the puzzle once sat was now just wood, wiped clean, cleared, plain. The cake had long since been cut quietly and eaten in small slices over several days, never with candles.

Life had settled into something that looked normal from the outside.

Normal, with one piece missing.

One Tuesday evening, about three weeks after my father left, the house was as usual. The TV murmured softly in the background, turned low. The sun had already dipped out of sight, but the last of its light still hung in the living room in a faint orange haze.

I sat at the table, pencil in hand, rewriting math problems I already understood. Numbers made sense. They followed rules. Show your work and you got credit even if you didn't get it right the first time.

People weren't like that.

From the kitchen, my mother rinsed and stacked dishes with a rhythm that sounded almost like a song without melody. Water on, water off. Cabinet open, cabinet closed. Plate, cup, bowl.

"Elijah," she called after a while, not turning around. "You almost done?"

"Yeah," I said. "Just checking it."

"Check it twice," she replied. "I don't want no surprises from that teacher of yours."

There was gentleness in her voice again. It had been coming back in little pieces, scattered through small moments, a joke here, a soft question there.

But her voice tired faster than it used to.

She cleared her throat more.

She drank water like she needed it.

I finished my last problem, closed my book, and sat back.

My mother dried her hands on a dish towel and glanced toward the cabinet above the fridge. Then, as if deciding with her whole body, she reached up and pulled down a small wooden box I hadn't seen in years with the tips of her fingers.

It was old, the grain worn smooth, the lid loose on its hinge. Childhood lived inside it.

She brought it to the table and sat down across from me.

"Do you remember this?" she asked.

I frowned, then opened the box.

Inside were small wooden shapes in primary colors. Circles. Squares. Triangles. Some odd shapes I never learned the names of, like a star that lost a point or a cloud with corners. The paint was chipped at the edges. Some had bite marks from when I was teething, she once told me.

"You used to carry these around everywhere," she said with a soft smile. "We couldn't go to the store without at least three of them in your pocket."

I picked up a blue rectangle and rolled it between my fingers. It felt lighter than I remembered.

"I forgot about these," I admitted.

"You grew out of them," she said. "That's what happens. Moved on to more complicated puzzles."

I looked at the large broken pieces of the sun, plush green hills, balloons floating within the blue cloud-ladened sky. Then, I thought of the empty spot at the table, our last puzzle together. Now it seemed like that spot had never held anything.

She watched me study the pieces and look toward the place my life shattered, her eyes gentle in a way I hadn't seen in weeks.

"You know why I kept these?" she asked interrupting my focus.

I shrugged. "Because you keep everything?"

She laughed, the sound small but real. "True. But these I kept on purpose."

She reached into the box, pulled out a small wooden shape that used to fit into a matching board. It looked like part of a balloon, something rounded with a little notch on the side.

"I was cleaning that hall drawer and found these pushed way in the back," she said. "I almost threw them out with the rest of the junk."

"Why didn't you?" I asked.

She turned the piece over in her fingers slowly, as if the answer was written on it.

"Because they reminded me of you," she said. "How you used to sit in the middle of the floor and make it your mission to figure out where everything went. You wouldn't get up until every hole had the right shape in it."

She looked at me.

"You never liked things out of place," she added quietly.

I looked down at the table. I didn't disagree.

She placed the piece in my open palm, then closed my fingers around it the way she had when I was much younger.

"Elijah," she said, voice steady now, "I want you to understand something."

I lifted my gaze.

"Life doesn't come together neat like those pictures on the boxes," she said. "You already know that now. So, I'm not going to pretend with you."

I swallowed, the shape warm in my hand.

"You're going to have days where it feels like whole pieces are missing," she continued. "You're going to have people walk out and parts of you will go with them. Things you thought would be permanent won't be. Things you thought would break you, may or may not."

She paused, letting the words breathe between us.

"But missing pieces don't mean the picture is ruined."

I looked at her. Really looked.

The tired lines around her eyes. The way her shoulders held tension and grace at the same time. She wasn't telling me a story to distract me. She was telling me the truth from inside her own hurt.

"So, what do I do?" I asked.

She smiled sadly. "You build what you can see," she said. "What's in front of you. One part at a time."

"That's what Dad said too," I replied quietly. "About puzzles. He always says, once the edges were set, the middle makes sense."

Something flickered across her face at the mention of him, but she didn't look away.

"Your daddy's good with edges," she murmured.

"What's that mean?" I asked.

She thought for a moment. "He knows how to set things up that look right. Job. House. Nice car. Outer frame stuff. And that's good."

She leaned forward slightly.

"But the middle's where the living is," she added. "And that part takes more than just putting pieces down. It takes intention, staying even when the picture doesn't look like the box."

Her words sank deeper than I could name.

"How do you know which pieces go in the middle?" I asked.

"You don't," she said. "Not all the time. Sometimes you just hold onto the ones you know fit and trust the rest will show up when it's time."

I stared at my hand.

"What if some never show up?" I asked.

Her eyes glossed, but she didn't let the tears fall. "Then you learn how to live with space," she said. "And you don't let that space tell you you're less than whole."

I went quiet.

She reached out and smoothed my hair.

"Your life is not broken because he left," she said. "Harder, maybe. Different, yes. But not broken."

I nodded.

"You're still you," she continued as she smiled. "You still have that brilliant mind that sees everything, that soft heart that feels deep, and a future that doesn't end at this house. Don't let this one part of the picture convince you that you're not worth finishing."

"I didn't finish the puzzle," I said.

"I know," she replied. "And that's alright."

"But, I thought you said to always finish what I start."

"Baby, some things finish the minute you decide it's done."

I hadn't thought about it that way.

It didn't make me feel better exactly.

But my mind was clearer.

She leaned back and exhaled.

"I can't fix what he did," she said. "I can't fill the space he left. I wish I could. But I can tell you this. You are not what happened to you and you are not done."

I held her gaze.

"You are who you choose to be now."

She paused, then added quieter, "And Elijah?"

"Yeah?"

"Don't ever rush your process. Even the sun doesn't hurry when it rises baby."

I frowned slightly. "But it always comes up."

She smiled. "Exactly."

The room was quiet again. But it wasn't empty.

In my hand, the small wooden shape warmed with my body heat.

"Can I keep this?" I asked.

She smiled. "It's yours. Always has been."

I put it in my pocket.

Later that night, lying in bed, I turned it between my fingers in the dark. The smoothness. The chipped edge. The way it fit in my palm.

My father's words drifted back to me. Get the edges right and the middle makes sense. My mother's words followed. The middle is where the living is.

I didn't know how those two truths would ever meet.

For now, I rested in the small understanding I had.

Eventually my hand relaxed, the refrigerator hummed as expected and sleep came without dreams.

Downstairs, the dining table sat bare and clean.

It would be a long time before I realized how deep that lesson went.

But the piece in my pocket stayed with me. And for now, that was enough.

The Music Stopped

I didn't notice the exact day childhood slipped away.

It didn't arrive with drama or ceremony, no clear moment I could point back to and say, *That was it.* It faded the way light fades from a room; slowly at first, then suddenly gone, leaving the corners in shadow. One day the world felt held, structured, predictable. The next it felt like something had shifted and no one had thought to tell me.

Middle school came with its own strange weather. Boys grew overnight, limbs too long for their bodies. Girls whispered in clusters I didn't understand yet, voices changing before faces did. Friends who used to trade snacks and talk about cartoons started sorting themselves into new categories. Loud ones. Mean ones. Confused ones.

I stayed observant.

Teachers liked me because I didn't disrupt class. I listened. I nodded. I answered when spoken to. They called me mature. They didn't know silence was easier than explaining everything happening inside me.

At recess I took a ball to the side court and shot alone. The rhythm steadied me - the thump of rubber on concrete, the clean arc of a shot, the sound of it falling through the net. No guessing. No betrayal. The court didn't change its mind. The rim didn't leave. It stayed where it was supposed to be and I made my home there.

Life was quieter than it used to be, almost predictable.

My mother got up early. She went to work. She paid bills and complained about the bills. She folded laundry, still fussed about homework, cooked when she had the energy, heated leftovers when she didn't. She moved like someone who had decided stopping was not an option.

When I think back on her from those years, my mother was still beautiful to me. Not in the way men talk about women, but in a way that felt familiar and permanent. She was small, delicate even. At 5'4 and barely 133 pounds, she seemed almost fragile.

Back then, I did not tower over her the way I would later. I was still growing into myself, still figuring out where my body ended and everything else began. But even now, standing at 6'2 and 187 pounds, I can still see her the way I saw her then.

Small.

But never weak.

She reminded me of that more than once.

"Just because you're bigger than me doesn't mean I won't chop you down to size if you ever try me."

It used to make me laugh to myself, not because I doubted her, but because I knew she meant it. There was a firmness in her that never needed volume. Her eyes carried both gentleness and resilience, the kind that had learned how to keep going even when it cost everything.

She looked tired most days, like it settled behind her eyes and lingered there.

There was a loneliness to it too, something quiet but visible, like a flower that had gone too long without water. Still standing. Still intact. Just not as full as it once was.

The biggest change showed up in the mornings.

She used to hum while she cooked. Old church songs, sometimes a little R&B from the radio. Every now and then she would move without thinking, just a small sway or a shoulder roll that made the kitchen feel warmer than it was. Those mornings had a rhythm to them, something soft and unspoken that made the house feel whole.

Then, at some point, it stopped.

The kitchen was not cold, just intentional.

Every movement had a purpose. The pan against the stove, the spoon against the pot, the cabinet opening and closing, the steady stream of water from the sink. Nothing extra. Nothing wasted.

No humming.

I noticed, but I never said anything.

At ten, you do not ask your mother why the music stopped. You learn how to live around the silence instead, how to accept it without disturbing it.

The years that followed did not arrive loudly. They settled in, one on top of the other, until the quiet no longer felt like something missing.

By the time I got older, I had grown used to it.

Eventually, she tried dating.

The first man looked enough like my father to bother me. Not in a way I could explain, just enough to make me skeptical. He had the same kind of shoulders, the same laugh that came out too loud and disappeared too fast. He brought flowers once. My mother smiled, thanked him, and placed them in water like it was something expected, not something she felt.

She did not keep seeing him, but I noticed she kept the flowers longer than I thought she should have.

Even after they started to wilt and died.

I never asked her why.

But every summer after that, once I started working, I made sure to buy her flowers every week so she would never feel the need to keep dead flowers around ever again.

There were men from church who always found reasons to extend conversations. Most of them pretended to be interested in me until they realized she was not interested in them. Coaches spoke to her longer than necessary after games, and even strangers seemed drawn to her without understanding why. She was not flashy or loud about herself. She did not need to be. She carried a presence that commanded attention without asking for it, and most people found themselves looking twice without knowing what had drawn them in.

She would smile, be polite, and move on.

I asked her once why she did not talk to any of them.

She laughed, soft but certain.

"Eli, never mess where you eat."

The few men she allowed close never stayed long. Something was always off. Too eager. Too distant. Too loud. Too something neither of us could quite name.

I did not like watching her try.

I liked it even less when it did not work.

There was something about seeing her moving on that unsettled me in a way I could not explain. It was not jealousy. It felt more like resistance, like something in me rejected the idea of her being with someone even though I knew she deserved to.

She cried sometimes.

Not often. Not loudly.

But I saw it.

Even when the tears did not fall, they showed up in her eyes, sitting just beneath the surface like they were waiting for permission.

People came and went.

I learned to expect that.

And each time it happened, something in me stretched a little further than it should have, leaving behind a space that never quite closed the same way again.

By the time I reached high school, I had started to believe I understood something about life. Or maybe I had just learned how to carry things without letting them show.

My shoulders broadened, and my voice settled into something lower, steadier. I moved with a calm people mistook for confidence. On the basketball court, I found something I did not need words for, a language that did not require explanation. Out there, I was not the boy with the missing father or the one watching his mother grow quieter by the year.

I was reliable. Necessary. Useful.

Coaches trusted me with the ball. Teammates trusted me with the play, and scouts began to show up more often than I expected. It felt like purpose, even if I never called it that.

Girls noticed me, too.

I learned how to recognize it without ever really responding to it. A look that lingered a second too long. Conversations that stretched beyond what they needed to be. The way some of them seemed comfortable around me, like my quiet meant something more than it actually did.

They called it calm. Said I was steady. Easy to be around.

Some of them liked that.

Some of them did not.

Some of them wanted more of me than I knew how to give, not in a way that felt demanding, just in a way that felt natural, like it was expected that you let people in, that you allow yourself to be known.

I did not understand how to do that.

One girl said something to me once that stayed with me longer than I expected. She looked at me, really looked, and said, "You hear me, but you don't let yourself be heard."

I knew she was right.

I just did not know what she expected me to do about it.

So I did what made the most sense at the time.

Nothing.

We ended the way people say they want to, peacefully, respectfully, without anything breaking on the surface. She cried. I held her while she did and told her she would be alright.

I believed that.

But standing there, holding someone who was breaking over something I could not fully feel, I noticed something I did not yet have the language for.

My heart did not follow me into moments like that.

It stayed back, uninvolved.

Senior year passed quietly, the same way everything else had. There was no defining moment, no sudden clarity, just time continuing forward until it began to feel like something was ending whether I acknowledged it or not.

College letters came in. My mother kept every single one, even the rejections, stacking them like they all carried equal weight.

Maybe to her, they did.

We did not talk about my father anymore. Not because it did not matter, and not because we forgot, but because life had filled the space he left so thoroughly that it no longer felt like an absence. It felt like routine.

Work. School. Responsibility.

The absence did not disappear. It just blended in.

The night before graduation, I sat on the porch steps and listened.

The neighborhood had its own rhythm. Cicadas humming like they always had. Porch lights flicking on one by one. Someone laughing in the distance. Someone else arguing like it was nothing new.

Life kept moving.

And I realized I was not really in it the way other people seemed to be.

I was close enough to see it and participate in it, but not close enough to be affected by it.

That realization did not disturb me.

It settled me.

It taught me something I never questioned, that attachment has a cost. Not all at once, not in a way you can point to, but over time it asks for pieces of you that you do not always get back.

Closeness creates expectations.

Expectations create disappointment.

And disappointment has a way of staying longer than anything else.

I did not want that.

Or maybe I just did not trust myself to survive it.

So I adjusted.

Quietly.

I decided I would need less. I would still be kind, still present, still someone people could rely on, but not in a way that made me dependent on anyone else.

I would stay connected, but not exposed. Close, but not invested. Present, but never entangled.

At the time, it did not feel like loss.

It felt like maturity, like this was what becoming a man was supposed to look like.

I did not realize I was building something I would not know how to take down.

Sitting there in the warm night air, listening to other people's lives unfold without ever really touching mine, I felt something that almost passed for peace.

And I told myself something I never questioned.

Do not trust anyone, and if I want anything in this life, I will get it myself.

I would leave no room for anything to be taken from me.

My mother was still there.

But that night, I became a man, or at least I believed I did.

I held onto that belief like it was wisdom, and I carried it with me, not realizing it was the very thing that would keep me from ever feeling whole.

Learned Distance

College was the first place where nobody knew me before I opened my mouth.

I arrived on campus as a blank slate, and something about that felt both freeing and dangerous.

The campus itself was alive in a way my neighborhood had never been. Students moved fast, coffee cups in hand, backpacks slung low, music drifting out of open dorm windows. Flyers layered every bulletin board of various clubs, protests, parties, causes. Everything felt urgent, like the world had somewhere important to be.

I adjusted slower, moved at my own pace.

I walked the pathways with quiet intention, taking everything in piece by piece. I learned which buildings echoed too loudly, which courtyards stayed warm the longest in the afternoon sun, which benches you could sit on alone without looking lonely. I didn't rush into anything. I'd learned a long time ago that observing first was safer than explaining later.

I didn't talk much in the first few weeks. Not because I lacked confidence, I carried myself well, but because I understood how quickly people decided who you were. I wanted to learn the rhythm of the place before stepping fully into it.

My roommate, Marcus, was the opposite of me in almost every way. Loud. Friendly. Always laughing. He made friends the way some people breathe, without effort, without thinking. On our first day, he slapped me on the back and said, "Buddy, you're way too serious. We're in college now. You gotta loosen up."

I smirked. "I'll work on it."

He grinned like he'd won something. "Good. I can help."

Somehow, our differences worked. My calm grounded him. His energy pulled me into conversations I certain I would've avoided. Slowly, I let my world expand, carefully but willingly. I joined a business organization because it looked good on paper. I signed up for intramural basketball because movement still steadied me. I sat in the front row of my classes - not to impress professors, but because focus had always been my refuge.

I took a part-time job in the campus mailroom. Sorting packages. Delivering paperwork. I liked the predictability of it. Orders came in. Orders went out. No hidden meaning. No emotional guessing. Things arrived where they were supposed to.

There was a girl in my economics class who sat two rows over.

She caught my attention - Amber.

I noticed her before she noticed me. She had a soft voice, intelligent eyes, and she always carried a book that was not on the syllabus. Fiction, poetry, stories that seemed heavier than anything assigned. Sometimes she would smile at me as we passed on the way out of class, small and unassuming. It took weeks before we said more than a few polite words to each other.

One afternoon, after class, she tapped my arm lightly.

"You're Elijah, right?"

I nodded. "Yeah."

"I'm Amber." She shifted the books in her arms. "You always walk like you're thinking five steps ahead."

I let out a quiet laugh. "I didn't know I walked like anything."

"You do," she said, not teasing. "It's intentional. Like you're already somewhere else before you arrive."

I didn't know how to respond to that, so I smiled. "Maybe."

She tilted her head slightly. "It's interesting."

We walked together toward the courtyard. Her presence wasn't overwhelming. She spoke softly, choosing her words carefully. She didn't flirt, not at first.

She observed the way I observed the world. It felt like a mirror turned slightly off-center. I wasn't familiar with that sort of attention, it was nice I suppose.

Our conversations grew naturally over the weeks that followed. Nothing heavy. Nothing demanding. We talked about her favorite café, my early-morning gym habits, her fear of thunderstorms, my habit of waking up before sunrise even when I didn't need to. Just details. Safe ones.

Eventually, she asked if I wanted to study together in the library. I surprised myself by saying yes. I usually worked alone, but something about her steadiness felt comfortable to sit with. She didn't press me to talk more than I wanted. She didn't ask questions that came with expectations attached. It was easy.

Too easy.

Weeks passed. I liked her laugh. She liked the way I listened. We started eating lunch together, walking to class together, sending late-night texts that didn't say much but somehow meant something anyway.

One evening, we sat beneath a tree near the dorms as the sky shifted from gold to deep blue. The conversation drifted from school to music to the kind of future we imagined for ourselves. Nothing forced. Nothing heavy.

She studied me for a moment before speaking. "You feel things deeply," she said quietly.

My chest tightened. "I do?"

She nodded. "Yeah. But you hold those feelings like you're afraid they'll take over if you let them out."

I looked away, pretending to watch a group of students laughing near the fountain. She didn't push.

"You don't have to explain anything," she added gently. "I just want you to know… you're safe with me. If you ever want to share more."

I nodded, didn't answer. I wasn't good at opening doors quickly. I never had been.

She reached for my hand and held it. She wasn't claiming or expecting, just offering. I let her.

Our relationship unfolded slowly after that. Study sessions. Shared meals. Long conversations that felt comfortable and familiar. She knew when I needed silence and respected it. I knew when she wanted closeness and offered it.

But I still kept something back.

A small but deliberate distance I didn't know how to close.

Amber never pushed. She let me set the pace. And I told myself that meant I was doing it right.

One night, after a long day, I sat alone in my dorm room and pulled the wooden shape from the drawer where I'd hidden it. I hadn't shown it to anyone. I wasn't sure why I'd brought it to college at all. Maybe to remind myself of what staying looked like. Maybe to guard against what leaving felt like.

I thought about Amber, how she made me laugh without trying, how she made me feel seen without demanding more than I could give. I thought about her patience, her quiet understanding.

I also thought about how much she deserved.

And how little I knew how to offer without risking myself.

I placed the wooden shape back in the drawer carefully, then lay back on my bed and stared at the ceiling. I told myself I was being wise. That restraint was maturity. That distance was discipline.

I didn't know it yet, but this was the first relationship where I could feel the tension between who I was becoming and who I was still afraid to be.

And just like every puzzle before, I started from the edges.

Careful. Controlled. Intentional.

The middle, though…

The middle was already asking more than I knew how to give.

And I was beginning to believe that keeping my distance wasn't avoidance.

It was survival.

New Pieces

Amber was never the kind of girl who demanded clarity before it arrived.

She didn't press for commitments or force emotional conversations into the quiet spaces I left alone. She moved gently through the world, the kind of gentle that made people open without realizing they were doing it. And because I noticed that about her, I stayed cautious.

Still, something about her steadiness was beginning to draw me into a place I hadn't been before.

Not quite vulnerable - but leaning that way.

Close enough to feel the possibility of something real.

Far enough to pull back if I needed to.

Our days found a rhythm. Morning study sessions. Late lunches between classes. Slow walks back to the dorms when the air cooled and the campus lights came on one by one. It wasn't love yet, not the kind people talk about in grand language - but it was something taking shape. Something with edges forming. Something with the potential for a middle, if I could ever bring myself to step there.

I kept telling myself not to overthink it. She wasn't asking for forever or for promises.

She was only asking me to show up.

And for a while, I did.

But patterns return when you're not paying attention.

It began quietly. I missed a text and took too long to respond. She invited me to the movies and I said I had studying to do. Sometimes it was true. Sometimes it wasn't. Sometimes the idea of closeness stirred something in my chest that felt too familiar - an ache I didn't have language for, only avoidance.

Amber noticed before I said anything.

One afternoon as we walked back from lunch, she bumped her shoulder lightly into mine.

"You've been quieter lately," she said.

Not accusing. Not insecure.

Just noticing.

"Long week," I replied.

She nodded. "Okay."

But her eyes lingered on me, seeing more than I wanted her to.

I looked away.

A few days later we sat in the library at our usual table. She tried to read, but I could feel her attention drifting toward me again and again. The weight of being seen settled uncomfortably on my shoulders.

I closed my laptop. "You good?"

She hesitated. "Yeah… I just feel like you're slipping away a little."

"I'm not," I said.

"You are," she replied softly. "Not dramatically. Just… piece by piece."

The words touched something in me - not sharply, but deeply. She was naming something I had perfected hiding. Something I had learned to do so well it felt like second nature.

She leaned forward, elbows on the table, chin resting in her hands.

"I'm not asking you to be anything other than who you are," she said. "I just want to know where I stand with you."

I nodded. "I hear you."

"But do you understand me?"

I didn't.

But I didn't want to hurt her.

"I'm not trying to disappear," I said quietly.

She gave a small, sad smile. "I know. That's what makes it confusing."

Two days later she asked me to go to a concert with her.

I told her I had a paper due.

She didn't argue. She just told me to have a good night.

I did have a paper due. But that wasn't why I didn't go.

After that, she became more careful with me. Not cold. Just gentler. Less reaching. More space.

I told myself I appreciated the freedom.

But the space felt heavier than closeness ever had.

One evening she invited me to meet her friends. I almost said yes. I could see how much it mattered to her. But something inside me tightened - old, instinctive, familiar.

I told her I wasn't feeling well.

She said she understood.

And she did.

That was the problem.

A week later we sat under the same tree where I had first held her hand.

This time she pulled her knees to her chest.

"Elijah," she said gently, "I think you're trying. But I don't think you're ready to let someone choose you."

"That's not true," I said.

She shook her head. "It's not a criticism. It's just where you are."

I let the silence settle.

"I care about you," she continued. "But you're still living from something that hurt you long before I ever met you. And I can't compete with a ghost."

The words landed heavier than I expected.

"I don't want to lose you," I said.

Her voice softened into something that felt like both kindness and goodbye.

"I don't want to lose you either. But I think I already am."

She stood.

"When you're ready to stop running," she said quietly, "you're going to be capable of something incredible. And whoever gets that version of you… she's going to be very lucky."

She walked away without looking back. I didn't follow.

I told myself it was because I respected her decision.

That I understood what she was saying and I wasn't going to force something that didn't fit.

That's what I told myself.

But the truth was deeper; I didn't know how to go after something I didn't know how to keep.

Keep Moving

I learned that endings don't always announce themselves.

Sometimes they happen quietly. A conversation that loosens something. A moment that tilts the ground just enough that you realize you're not standing where you were before.

With Amber, the ending wasn't loud. There were no raised voices, no slammed doors, no broken promises. It simply settled. Like dust in a room no one visits anymore.

The days after she walked away felt hollow in a way I didn't expect.

I wasn't heartbroken. Not in the way people talk about heartbreak. I didn't lose sleep. I didn't lose focus. But something in me felt off balance, like a screw had been loosened somewhere I couldn't reach.

I went to class.

I ate.

I lifted weights.

I laughed when appropriate.

Life kept moving. It just felt flatter.

Marcus noticed.

He always did.

One afternoon he was digging through our mini fridge, looking for something that resembled food. He paused mid-search and looked over his shoulder at me.

"Bro… why do you look like somebody unplugged your soul?"

I glanced up from my laptop. "I'm fine."

"You're lying," he said, pointing a yogurt cup at me like it was evidence. "You're walking around like you're in a documentary called *The guy who lost it all*."

I laughed despite myself. "Bro. Relax."

"It's Amber, ain't it."

I didn't answer.

He grabbed two bottles of water, tossed one at me, and sat on the edge of his bed.

"You wanna talk about it?"

"Nope."

"You gonna talk about it anyway."

"No."

Marcus leaned back. "Alright. Then I'm just gonna guess."

I shook my head.

"She finally got tired of your mysteriously aloof charm, didn't she?"

I didn't deny it.

Marcus's tone softened. "You a good dude. But you hold people like they fragile. Or like you scared you might drop 'em."

I leaned back in my chair. "Maybe I am."

He studied me. "Or maybe you scared they'll drop you."

The words landed heavier than he intended.

We didn't say much after that.

He didn't need to.

The truth had been named.

The next few days settled into a rhythm I didn't resist.

I worked out harder.

Ran later.

Buried myself deeper in assignments.

Anything that made my mind quieter.

Still, Amber's absence hovered around me like a faint echo.

I saw her sometimes. Always kind. Always calm. Always moving forward.

She never made me feel like I'd done something wrong.

That somehow made it worse.

One evening I passed a table in the quad where volunteers were collecting donations for displaced families. A young lady smiled and handed me a pamphlet.

"Anything helps."

Her voice was sweet. Simple. Genuine.

I gave a few dollars.

As I walked away, something shifted quietly in me.

Maybe the world was full of people I hadn't met yet.

Maybe every connection wasn't meant to last and existed only to show you something about yourself.

Back in my room, I took and quick shower and opened my drawer. The wooden shape seemed to pop out like a reminder.

I stood there. For a quick moment, I thought of my pops. Good times.

Picking the piece up, I traced the edges realizing how much has changed and what hasn't.

It wasn't lost, it wasn't broken. Just disconnected.

And for the first time, I wondered if healing wasn't just about finding someone to fill a space.

Maybe it was about the intention to willingly connect to something.

I closed the drawer gently.

Some things don't come together at all at once.

Some things take time.

Last Words

I didn't set out to become someone new.

It happened in small adjustments. Quiet disciplines repeated until they hardened into habit, then into structure, then into something that began to shape me while I was too busy moving to notice. I didn't know exactly where I was headed, but I understood systems. I understood momentum. I knew how to keep my head down and get things done.

Then one day I looked up and realized I wasn't standing in the same place anymore.

I was standing in a stadium, cap and gown on my shoulders, applause rolling across the crowd like weather moving in.

Graduation felt bigger than the moment itself. Cameras flashed. Families leaned forward, shouting names that suddenly sounded larger than the people who carried them. The loudspeakers echoed each one with ceremony, stretching ordinary lives into something that felt important.

When they called mine, I walked across the stage steady and sure.

I didn't rush. Didn't look around. Just focused on the steps in front of me.

I already had an offer waiting in Dallas, Texas. A good job, with relocation covered and an apartment arranged. Within two weeks and I would be Chicago.

Everything was lined up.

For the first time in a long time, the future didn't feel uncertain.

It felt engineered.

I didn't know how to perform excitement. I never had. Instead, I took moments in quietly, the way you take a breath and hold it a second longer than necessary.

In the stands, my mother sat with her hands folded in her lap.

She was smiling, but it wasn't the kind of smile people wear for pictures. It carried something heavier. Pride, yes. But also relief. Years of working double shifts. Years of stretching groceries, stretching sleep, stretching herself thinner than she ever admitted.

She looked older than she should have.

But when our eyes met, her face softened into something so full it pressed against my chest from a distance.

After the ceremony, she found me near the edge of the crowd and wrapped her arms around my shoulders.

She held on longer than most people do.

"You did it," she whispered.

I hugged her back. "So did you."

She pulled away, laughing softly. "I just showed up."

"No ma, you stayed," I said. "You got me here. That's different."

She didn't argue.

We sat in the car afterward with the windows down. Warm air drifting in, carrying the smell of cut grass and asphalt and summer beginning. The noise from the stadium faded behind us.

For a while, neither of us said anything. We didn't need to.

Then she spoke.

"You have great things ahead of you, son. Don't rush your process. Savor every moment."

I smiled. "You say that all the time, Mom."

"Then remember it," she said. "And please, build something that lets you breathe."

She leaned across the console and hugged me again.

This time she held tighter.

Then she pulled back, her eyes bright again, her voice lighter.

"Send me a cowboy hat," she said. "I've always wanted one."

I laughed. "It's Dallas, ma. I doubt they're handing those out. But if I find one, I'll send you the hat and the boots to match. How about that?"

Her face lit up. "I can't wait! The whole neighborhood will be jealous."

Then the smile faded a little.

"I'm going to miss you," she said quietly. There were tears in her eyes now.

"Ma, don't cry," I said gently. "I'm a phone call away. I'll be back. And you can come visit me."

"I know," she said, nodding once, steadying herself the way she always did.

Then she took a breath and straightened up.

"Now let's go eat."

She was good at that.

Knowing exactly when a moment had gone deep enough.

That was the last full conversation we ever had.

***

Seven months later, a call came.

It was late. One of those long days that blurred into itself, meeting stacked on meeting, decisions layered on decisions. I had just closed the largest acquisition in our company's history. Everyone had shaken my hand. Numbers had aligned. Strategy had paid off and talks of a promotion was on the horizon.

I was still sitting behind my desk, basking in the glory of the dividends when the office phone rang.

The receptionist had already left.

I almost let it go to voicemail, but the area code caught my attention. Home.

I didn't recognize the number.

I picked up, didn't quite understand the words at first.

But I understood the tone; that careful gentleness people use when they're about to fracture something inside you.

I dropped everything and caught the first flight home.

***

The hospital was too bright for that hour.

White lights. No shadows. Everything flattened into the same pale color. The air smelled sharp and sterile and wrong, like something had been cleaned too thoroughly to feel human.

She looked smaller in the bed than I had ever seen her.

My mother had always filled a room without trying. Movement. Warmth. Presence.

Now she was still.

Machines kept rhythm where her body used to. Tubes ran across her arms like quiet questions no one was answering.

When her eyes opened and found me, relief came first.

"Hey baby," she said.

My throat tightened. "Hey."

I took her hand.

It didn't feel like her hand.

Lighter. Fragile in a way that didn't make sense.

"I'm okay," she said. "I just need you to listen."

I nodded.

She studied my face the way she always had - like she was memorizing it for later.

"I love you so much, Eli. Everything I did… was to make sure you became a good man."
Her voice thinned, but didn't break.
"I got to see that. I'm the happiest woman in the world."

Something in me resisted that.

"Ma… what's going on?"

She didn't hesitate.

"Cancer, baby."

The word didn't land.

It moved past me. Like it belonged to someone else's life.

"What?" My voice came out sharper than I expected. My hand pulled away before I realized it. "Cancer? When? What do you mean cancer?"

She stayed calm.

Too calm.

"I've been fighting for a while. I saw you graduate. I saw you get your job. I saw you build your life. That's what I wanted."

The room shifted.

Not dramatically. Just enough to make everything feel off balance.

"How long?" I asked.

She paused.

"A few years."

For a second, I didn't understand the language.

Then I did.

"A few years?"
My voice broke - this time I couldn't control it. "You let me leave? You let me move across the country while you were sick?"

"Baby," she said softly, "you were building your future. I wasn't going to pull you backward."

That didn't feel like love.

It felt like distance.

Or maybe it felt like the same thing I had been doing my whole life, letting things go before they could hold me.

I took her hand again.

Carefully this time.

Like I could undo what had already happened if I held it right.

"I'm here," I said.

I really didn't know what that meant.

She smiled at me.

The same smile she's held my entire life that said – everything is okay.

But this time, it wasn't.

"Elijah," she said, "no matter what happens, I'm always with you. You understand that?"

I did not understand. But, I nodded because I couldn't say no.

I couldn't ask her not to leave.

Somehow, a part of me already felt braced for this – another loss.

I rested my head against her leg and stayed there.

Long enough for her breathing to slow. Long enough for the machines to take over the rhythm of the room.

I didn't cry.

I didn't pray.

I didn't ask for more time.

I just stayed.

My mother passed two days later.

The world did not pause.

Phones still rang. Traffic still moved. Coffee still brewed. People laughed on sidewalks, while something inside me collapsed in slow motion.

Planning her funeral felt unnatural.

Like I was organizing something for someone who had only stepped out for a moment.

She prepared everything beforehand. Left exact instructions in a folder listing everything from preferred flower arrangements, songs…all the way to the casket color and burial plot.

A plan.

She had always taken care of things.

It made the process easier. It didn't make it lighter.

By the time I arrived at the church, the doors were already open.

The sanctuary smelled like lilies and old wood and something sweet I couldn't name. People filled the pews, their voices low, respectful. Neighbors. Church friends. Coworkers.

People who knew parts of her I never would.

I sat in the front row and stared at the casket.

I felt nothing and everything at the same time, like something inside me had shut down just enough to keep me upright.

That's when my father appeared.

I knew it was him before I turned. There are some things your body remembers even when your mind tries not to. The weight of his presence. The space he took up without asking.

He sat beside me, shoulder to shoulder, like he had never left.

"Elijah," he said quietly. "I'm sorry."

The words landed, but they didn't settle.

I could not look at him.

I stayed where I was for a second longer, then stood and walked to the casket instead. It felt easier to face something that did not speak back.

I stood there long after the service ended. Long after the room emptied. Long after the last voices faded into the hallway.

Eventually, I felt him behind me again.

Not close enough to touch.

Just close enough to remind me he was still there.

"I made a lot of mistakes, son," he said. "Don't be like me."

I turned then.

Not because I was ready, but because I needed to see him.

For a second, I did not see a stranger.

I saw something familiar. The same eyes. The same frame I had grown into. The same presence I had spent years learning how to replace.

It unsettled me in a way I had not expected.

There were questions I could have asked him.

Where were you…Why did you leave….Did you ever think about us?

But none of them made it past my chest.

Because standing there, looking at him, I realized something I had never said out loud.

I had already answered those questions for myself.

It was in the way I refused to need anything from anyone who could leave.

He nodded once, like he understood something I had not said.

Then he walked away.

Again.

***

A week later, I sat alone in my mother's house.

Every room held her. Not just the big memories, but the small ones - the way she folded towels, the faint scent of her soap, the quiet order she kept as if holding life together one surface at a time.

I stood at the bottom of the stairs and, without warning, another image settled over the space.

Duffel bags.
The day my father left.

For a moment I could see them again, sitting where he'd dropped them, the air heavy with something no one had words for.

Sometimes I wonder if that was the beginning of her wearing down. Carrying the weight of two on one set of shoulders. Holding the house, the bills, the silence, and me.

That kind of strength looks steady from the outside.

From the inside, it costs.

I went into her bedroom and knelt beside the bed. My hand brushed against something tucked underneath.

The shoebox that held my favorite childhood puzzle.

Perfect condition, every piece in place. Untouched. Preserved like it was waiting for something.

I stared at it for a long moment.

Then I stood, walked to the center of the room –

and threw it.

The box hit the wall and burst open. Wooden pieces scattered across the floor, skidding into corners, sliding under furniture, breaking the picture apart again.

"Why would you lie to me?" I yelled into the empty room.

The first words I had spoken in days.

"You were sick. For years. You let me leave. You let me build a life while you were dying."

I sat down on her bed.

Her pillow was still there. White lace edging. The one she always used.

It still smelled like her.

I lay down in her space and pulled the pillow to my face, breathing in slowly, like I could hold her there if I didn't move. I stayed like that for hours, until I fell asleep.

At some point the sun disappeared and the room darkened.

Sitting up abruptly, I looked around as if I had just woken up from a bad dream. But it was real…too real.

I went back to the floor and picked up every scattered piece.

One by one and placed them back in the box.

Then I put the box of broken pieces in my luggage.

I didn't know it yet.

But I'd begin carrying that brokenness with me.

Emily

When I returned to the city, I didn't come back the same.

I came back quieter.
Numb in places I didn't examine.

But somehow sharper.
More deliberate and purposely efficient.

I sold my mother's house. I couldn't bear the thought of it standing somewhere without me, holding her in spaces neither of us would ever walk again.

I packed her things carefully; folded her clothes, boxed her books, labeled everything like order could keep loss from spreading. As if naming the objects might preserve what they meant.

Then I went back to work. Immediately.

Work welcomed me without hesitation.

Deadlines didn't grieve. Meetings didn't pause. Spreadsheets balanced. Flights boarded. Contracts closed. The world moves easily for people who refused to stop moving.

So, I didn't.

His face stayed with me - my father's.

It looked like mine, only older, marked by lines I hadn't earned yet. Evidence of the bridges that were never built between us. We shared the same structure, the same eyes. I had heard it my whole life - *you look just like him.*

I never knew what to do with that.

Standing beside him at the funeral, it didn't feel like I was seeing him. It felt like I was being confronted with something I didn't want to become.

Or worse… something I already was.

Don't be like me.

He left the words behind like a sign without direction.

My mother never mentioned the resemblance. Not once. I know she saw it - every time she looked at me. Yet she never held it against me, and she never let his absence shape the way she loved me.

Still, the thought stayed with me.

Every day without her took effort. She was in every conversation and every quiet moment.

So, I kept moving forward…faster.

Motion felt safer than memory.

And then one afternoon, without warning -

I saw her.

Emily.

Stopped me cold in my tracks.

It wasn't just how she looked. It was the way she held space. She knew exactly how to own a room and let everything else fall in line around her.

Emily has an ornamental beauty- striking, confident, contained.. The kind of woman you'd see in a catalogue and then see again in real life and realize the catalogue hadn't done her justice.

We had already noticed each other.

Weeks of passing in the lobby. Glances in meetings we didn't belong in. That quiet recognition that lives somewhere between curiosity and permission.

She knew I saw her.

And she let me.

One morning, I stepped onto the elevator just before the doors closed. She slipped in behind me, a folder sliding from her arm.

Papers scattered across the floor.

We bent at the same time. Our hands met over the folder.

She didn't pull away.

She looked at me - slow, deliberate - and smiled.

Something in me moved.

Something I hadn't felt move in a long time.

She asked for my number.

No harm in that.

I suggested happy hour.

No hesitation.

No buildup.

As the elevator doors opened, she turned slightly. "Six o'clock. The Olivet."

"I know it," I said.

"I figured you would," she smiled. "See you then."

The Olivet. Invite only.

That told me everything I needed to know - only the best with her, I liked that.

Dinner unfolded easily, banter slipping into laughter, laughter easing into quiet unspoken touches that were clearly understood.

She wasn't heavy with conversation, didn't pry or reach for anything beneath the surface. Everything about her stayed light, intentional.

She talked about travel, scrolling through pictures of beaches and sunsets, the glow of distant places reflecting off her skin in a way that made it hard not to notice. Every image seemed to hold her just right, like the world had been arranged around her without effort.

And I couldn't deny it, this girl was fine.

She didn't wait for me to make the next move.

She didn't need to, I was more intoxicated with her than with the three bottles of Chateau Lafite finished between us.

"I'm not ready for the night to end," she said easily. "Your place or mine? I just bought this ridiculously large television and I'm dying to watch it with someone."

I smiled. "Raincheck on the television. My place."

I had an unspoken rule. I don't go to a woman's house until after a few dates. I prefer my own environment.

She didn't hesitate. She slipped into her coat without taking her eyes off me.

The moment the door to my penthouse closed behind us, everything shifted.

There was no pause, no transition into something softer or more intentional.

Just movement, immediate and certain.

She stepped into me like she had already decided where the night was going, and I met her there without resistance. My hands found her, firm, unhesitating, pulling her closer in a way that left no space between intention and action.

She responded just as quickly.

No hesitation. No restraint.

There was something raw about it, something unfiltered. The kind of connection that didn't reach for meaning because it didn't need it. It existed entirely in the moment, in the physical closeness, in the rhythm that formed without conversation.

And I didn't hold anything back.

I didn't measure the moment.

I didn't create distance.

I was fully present in it.

Completely.

Our passion was unbridled.

There was no need for food when we were together.

She was the meal.

Warm and consuming.

Time blurred as the night dissolved into morning.

She approached the front door with her heels in her hand, her hair undone, her expression relaxed in a way that suggested nothing needed to be explained.

She paused, turned and said, "That was incredible. See you tonight?"

I smiled, looking down and then back up. He seemed to agree before I did. "I'll pick up dinner."

"No need," she said. "I already have plans. Ten?"

That landed differently.

But it was better this way.

No strings. I really just needed the release.

"Yeah." I said.

She carefully put on her shoes and left.

I lay back down, hoping for an hour of sleep, but her perfume still lingered in the sheets. As pleasant as it was, I never played the risk game. She may not show and I had Sabrina or Chelsea always on standby when I wanted company. I couldn't stand being alone at night. Mom would always visit my dreams.

I stripped the bed, washed the linens, replaced them, and went to work.

Order restored.

Days with Emily followed the same pattern.

She couldn't seem to get enough.

When I left my office for the evening, she was leaving hers. Our worlds aligned without effort, but I was intent to never mistake that for meaning.

It was just human nature.

We didn't pretend it was more than it was.

We agreed not to dig.
No expectations. No future language. No vulnerability required.

It was clean.
It was easy and I kept it loose.

Emily became the place my pain went when it needed somewhere warm, with no pressure to land. She felt like a frequent vacation.

She didn't heal me but she did distract me from reality.

She enjoyed how much I gave without needing what I kept.

I gave freely, knowing it wouldn't require anything deeper in return.

It worked.

Until it didn't.

Until I noticed that what I was avoiding wasn't the past, it was me.

That realization didn't arrive dramatically.

It arrived the way real things often do.

In a pause, a breath. In a moment where nothing was wrong, yet nothing felt right either.

And that's when I understood something I had never allowed myself to name:

I wasn't afraid of loss; I'd lived with it much of my life.

I was afraid of what would surface if I ever stopped long enough to feel it.

And somewhere between the man I had become and the boy I had been - between the edges I kept building and the middle I kept avoiding, something was missing.

I missed my mother and I was alone in the world. That was my truth. And I wasn't ready to deal with that yet.

Life Happens

The promotion came with a corner office, a salary increase impressive enough to make my colleagues blink twice, and a title people twice my age were still chasing.

I accepted it the way I accepted everything else.

Calm. Composed. No celebration. Just a firm handshake that said I understood the responsibility, and everything that would be expected of me moving forward.

My days grew longer after that. My influence expanded, and my calendar filled itself with strategy meetings, executive briefings, and dinners where conversation was split evenly between networking and performance. I moved through it all with ease. I listened more than I spoke. I read rooms before I entered them. I understood what people meant even when they chose not to say it out loud.

It impressed people.

It didn't surprise me.

I had been building toward this long before I knew what to call it, back when I learned to focus on surfaces and edges before ever touching the middle.

Structure felt safer than chaos.

Order felt kinder than emotion.

The higher I climbed, the more noticeable the silence in my personal life became.

I had colleagues. Associates. Acquaintances. People who respected me. People who needed me. People who, in one way or another, wanted something from me.

But I did not have anyone I could be unguarded with.

Some nights, I stood in front of the windows in my penthouse, looking out over the city as it moved beneath me like something alive. Thousands of people in motion at once, loving, losing, breaking, healing, starting over.

I watched them the way you watch a place you are no longer part of.

Emily had come into my life like a spark.

Bright. Immediate. Impossible not to notice.

And just as quickly, she was gone.

Nothing dramatic happened. Nothing broke. We did not hurt each other.

She just began to lean in before I was ready to stop moving, and whenever I feel that kind of pull, something in me creates distance without asking.

A trip here.

A late meeting there.

Space disguised as ambition.

She noticed. Of course she did.

She softened first, became quieter in the way she spoke to me, more careful in the way she reached. She never confronted me. She adjusted instead.

And eventually, we both let things fade back into what they had been before we met.

After that, I buried myself deeper into work.

***

Marcus stopped by every now and then, usually on weekends.

One Saturday, he walked into my living room, paused, and slowly looked around.

"You ever gonna put something on these walls, man?" he said. "Feels like you live in a magazine."

I shrugged. "I thought you came to grill."

"Oh, I did," he said, already moving toward the kitchen. "I'm just saying… it's empty."

"It's maintained."

He glanced back at me. "It's lonely. You just don't want to call it that."

I poured myself a drink and let the comment pass without a response.

He watched me for a moment before speaking again. "You ever think about dating again?"

"I'm not avoiding it."

"Yes, you are," he said, easy and certain. "All those fine women at your job? No way I'd be single."

"They're coworkers. I don't mess where I eat. I was talking to someone in the building, but it wasn't anything serious."

"Respect," he said. "But what about women outside of work?"

I didn't answer.

Marcus leaned back, arms crossed, studying me the way people do when they already think they know the truth. "You can't keep acting like relationships are the plague. That's part of being human."

My jaw tightened just enough for me to feel it. "I've got ninety-nine problems," I said, lifting my glass of imported scotch slightly, "and a woman isn't one."

We both laughed.

"Trust me," I added. "I'm good."

He tilted his head. "Then why are you always by yourself?"

I turned toward the window, watching the city stretch into streaks of gold and white. "Same reason you are," I said. "Choice."

He shook his head. "Speak for yourself. I'm not single by choice. I want a family. Just haven't found the right one yet."

Before I could stop it, the answer came from somewhere deeper than I intended.

"Neither have I."

He paused, then let out a short laugh. "Look at us. Two successful men, women everywhere, and we still can't find one worth bringing home to momm…"

He stopped himself.

"Oh," he added quietly. "Sorry man…"

"It's cool," I said, steady. "I'm not really concerned about that. Doesn't get much better than this."

I lifted my glass again, letting the amber catch the light. "No stress."

Marcus watched me for a moment longer than usual, like he was trying to decide whether to believe me.

Then he nodded.

"Yeah," he said. "I hear you."

We made a few loose plans for the week, and a few minutes later he was gone.

Marcus always had a way of helping me keep things in perspective.

When the door closed behind him, I stood there for a moment, debating whether to take a nap or call someone over for a late-night snack. My hand reached for my phone automatically.

But the silence seemed to be watching me.

I lowered my hand and glanced down my hallway.

The door at the end stood closed – I rarely opened it unless I needed to break the monotony of my life.

I walked toward it slowly.

For a second, my hand rested on the knob.

Then I turned it.

The room felt the same as always. Still. Curated. Frozen in time.

The unfinished puzzles waited on the table.

I drifted toward one of them.

Emily – bright, colorful. I barely made it past the bottom edge.

There was Sabrina. Chelsea. Gabriella. Liz. Carla…dozens more.

Every box had a name. Every puzzle had a face. Every one captured a beginning that never became anything more.

I didn't keep them because I couldn't let go.

I kept them because they told the truth.

Each one marked the exact moment I stopped trying.

The moments I chose safety instead of depth.

They weren't trophies. They were evidence.

Proof that relationships were the one thing I couldn't seem to get right.

I stood there longer than I meant to.

There had been a time when I thought completion meant something had finally worked.

Now, I wasn't so sure.

Maybe I had only ever chosen puzzles I knew I could walk away from.

The next thought came quietly. What would it feel like to finally finish?

Not just the puzzle.

But me.

***

Later that evening my phone buzzed. A reminder about the gala I agreed to a few weeks back.

Reluctantly, I went.

The ballroom looked exactly like every other one I'd ever walked into - crystal chandeliers casting warm light over gold linens, soft jazz moving through the air, conversations polished into performance.

I slipped into the rhythm easily.

Handshake. Smile. Small talk. Charm.

Confidence came naturally. Presence non-intentional.

After an hour of moving through people without actually being with any of them, I stepped onto the terrace for air.

"Elijah."

I turned at the sound of my name.

One of my board members stood near the railing, a woman beside him.

"Elijah, I want you to meet someone," he said. "This is Maya. She's consulting with us on the new initiative."

I looked at her and immediately noticed what she wasn't doing.

She wasn't leaning in, wasn't performing, wasn't studying my reaction.

She wasn't trying to impress me.

She was simply standing there - calm, attentive, completely at ease in her own space.

Graceful. Observant. Grounded.

For the first time that night, the moment didn't feel like a stage.

She wore her dress with simplicity - a pearl pendant resting at her collar with matching earrings framing her face. Her quiet demeanor felt like an adornment of its own, worn the way others wear confidence.

There was something about her that stirred a sense of familiarity - something I recognized, though I didn't yet have a name for it.

"It's nice to meet you," she said.

"Maya," I replied. "Likewise."

That was it.

No rush.
No spark.
No urgency.

Just a strange curiosity that settled in me, slow and steady.

She gave a small nod when someone called her name, then turned and walked back inside.

She didn't linger or try to extend the moment. Didn't leave a trail of energy behind her.

Just a sense of calm.

Clarity.

I stayed on the terrace longer than I meant to.

For the first time in a long while, my thoughts weren't racing ahead of the moment. I wasn't planning, predicting, or positioning myself for what came next.

I was exactly where I was supposed to be.

And somewhere beneath the moment, something inside me had taken notice.

A subtle recognition.

Something about her felt familiar.

Like a place I hadn't realized I'd been looking for - she felt like home.

Maya

Maya wasn't the kind of woman who walked into a room expecting to be noticed. She carried herself with an easy certainty, an unrehearsed confidence of someone who didn't need attention to confirm she belonged.

It made people notice her anyway.

I felt it the moment we were introduced - before she said more than a few words.

The terrace settled into a calm stillness after the introductions. Not awkward. Not forced. Just the kind of quiet that didn't ask to be filled, as if neither of us felt the need to push the moment forward.

She moved to the railing and rested her hands along the edge, her gaze drifting over the skyline.

She wasn't looking at it the way people usually do -detached, distracted or half-heartedly impressed without really seeing. There was something softer in her expression. Something present. Almost like wonder.

I found myself noticing more than I intended.

The faint curve of her collarbone where the light rested against her skin. The way the breeze lifted a strand of her hair and she tucked it behind her ear without thinking. The way she moved without effort, without performance—graceful because she wasn't trying to be.

A subtle scent lingered around her. Clean. Warm. Sweet, not quite perfume. More like citrus, skin, and air after rain.

The kind of scent your body remembers because you can't find it everywhere.

"It's beautiful from up here," she said.

"It is," I replied. "Though I forget to look sometimes."

She angled her head toward me, studying me briefly. "That sounds like something a person says when they've been working too hard."

I smirked. "You get that from one sentence?"

"I get that from the way you loosened your tie like it owes you money."

I laughed. The sound surprised me. It came out easier than expected, like something that had been waiting for permission.

She smiled as if she felt it too.

"So," I said, "what brings you out here? You don't strike me as someone hiding from small talk."

"Oh, I am," she said easily. "Hiding, avoiding, pretending to be deeply invested in air molecules. Whichever looks the least antisocial."

I chuckled again. "Not a fan of these events?"

"I'm a fan of events." she said simply. "Just not the eventful performance of people."

She spoke with her hands. Not dramatically - just little movements that carried her thoughts forward. Open palms. Small circles. Gentle emphasis.

It caught me off guard how much I was watching her.

My mother used to talk with her hands.

I hadn't thought about that in a while.

"You're here for work?" I asked.

"Sort of. A friend dragged me. I work with the community outreach group. Nothing fancy. We partner with organizations sometimes, and this gala invited donors and affiliates."

"Which group?"

She told me. I recognized it.

"You're the first person tonight who didn't lead with their title and résumé."

She shrugged. "My résumé isn't who I am. It's just proof I survived a bunch of things I didn't enjoy."

That landed somewhere quiet and deep.

"So why are you out here?" she asked. "Don't tell me you're networking with the moon."

"I needed a break."

"From?"

She didn't push.

She didn't soften it. She just waited.

The room buzzed around us. Music floated faintly through the open doors behind us. Her essence felt like a pause in a sentence I'd been rushing through my whole life.

"Everything," I admitted.

She nodded. Not with pity. Not with curiosity. Just understanding.

"That tracks." she said leaning against the railing beside me, close enough that I felt the warmth of her without touching her. Close enough that my body registered her before my mind did.

After a moment she smiled again. "Also, I'm convinced the air inside is artificially perfumed with desperation."

I laughed. "You're not wrong."

"I know," she said. "It's a talent."

"You're different," I said before I could stop myself.

"So are you," she replied. "Most people here talk like they're auditioning for something. You talk like you're tired of pretending."

I didn't know how she saw that so quickly. It unsettled me in a way that felt honest.

"So," she said lightly, "tell me something true."

"True?"

"Something simple. Something honest."

I wasn't used to women asking for truth without asking for more.

"My life is good. Perfect, really. Yet it feels like a piece is missing sometimes," I said slowly. "Do you ever feel like that, Miss Maya?"

She nodded. "Of course. I've just learned to stop looking for what's missing where everyone else is looking."

Our eyes held for a moment before she turned back toward the horizon.

"And where should I look?" I asked.

She smiled. "Anywhere that feels like peace. Just don't rush the process."

I froze.

My mother used to say that.

The words lodged somewhere behind my ribs, like a memory I hadn't touched in years had just brushed past me.

Then her phone buzzed.

She glanced at it and sighed. "My ride's here. And I promised my dog I'd be home before the street lights come on. I'm late."

"You have a dog?" I asked, smiling.

"Yes. Bruno. King of shedding. Destroyer of shoes. Loyal companion. Very dramatic when ignored."

"Sounds intense." I said, now laughing.

"Only on days ending in Y."

She stepped back. "It was nice meeting you, Elijah."

"You too."

She turned to leave, then paused.

"You should look at the city more," she said. "It's hard to feel empty when you're staring at something filled with life."

She didn't wait for a response.

The noise swallowed her as she stepped back inside.

I stayed on the terrace long after she disappeared.

Not replaying her words.

But replaying her face, the way my body softened around her.

The way my breath had slowed.

The way my mind had stopped sprinting ahead.

I didn't know why she felt like clarity instead of chemistry.

I didn't know why my chest felt lighter and more awake at the same time.

I only knew this.

Something in me woke up.

And for the first time in a long time…

I wasn't running from the feeling. I stood with it.

A Different Piece

A few weeks passed.

Days folding into each other the way they always did. Meetings. Flights. Dinners that were more obligation than appetite. Evenings that ended with the same quiet and the same view.

I hadn't thought about her constantly. But she crossed my mind in small, inconvenient ways.

I didn't chase the feeling or try to name it. I simply let it exist, the way you do when something hasn't asked anything of you yet.

It was a Saturday morning when it happened.

I was dressed down, ball cap pulled low, dark aviators, coffee in hand. No suit. No posture. No expectation of being recognized. I liked mornings like that - anonymous, unclaimed, camouflaged.

She was walking toward me, phone in one hand, tote slung over her shoulder, moving at an unhurried pace that suggested she wasn't late but also wasn't killing time. Harmony. That's what struck me first. She walked in complete harmony, like a soft beat guided her.

She passed me without slowing.

I stopped.

Turned back.

"Maya?" I called her name as she stopped in her tracks as if she was trying to place my voice.

Her eyes searched my face for a second longer than politeness required.

"Elijah?"

I lifted my sunglasses just enough to smile. "Hey there."

Recognition softened her expression, followed by something warmer — amusement, maybe. Curiosity.

"Oh," she said, almost laughing. "You look different."

"So do you," I replied.

She studied me for a second. "Yea?"

"In a good way, I didn't realize your height."

That made her smile. A real one. Not performative. "Short, without those heels, huh?"

Before I knew it I responded, "No, perfect."

We stood there for a moment, the city moving around us, traffic humming, people weaving past. It didn't feel awkward or charged….just natural. Like two people pausing on the same page without trying to write ahead.

"This can't be a coincidence," she said lightly.

"Statistically, it could be," I answered.

She laughed. "You sound like someone who doesn't believe in chance."

"I believe in patterns," I said. "Chance just likes to pretend it isn't one."

She considered that. "That's unsettling."

"Where are you headed?" I asked.

The exchange lingered. Easy. Unforced. We talked briefly, how the morning felt - nothing personal, nothing revealing. Just enough to confirm that the first conversation hadn't been imagined.

Then her phone buzzed.

She glanced down, exhaled softly, the way someone does when responsibility taps them on the shoulder.

"I should go," she said. "I'm already late picking up Bruno."

"Of course."

She stepped back, adjusting her bag, then paused again.

"It was good seeing you."

"You too, Maya."

She turned to walk away, then glanced back one last time.

"See you around."

Something in me moved suddenly and before I could reason myself out of it, I spoke. "Maya."

She turned.

I hesitated for half a beat, surprised by myself.

"Do you mind if I call you?"

She didn't react the way most people do.

There was no flattery, no discomfort, no calculation. Just thoughtfulness. She took a moment, considering not me but herself.

"I don't give out my number," she said honestly. "Not because I'm disinterested. I'm just careful about where I place access."

I nodded. That made sense to me in a way I couldn't explain.

"But," she added, "Maybe we'll meet again, if chance isn't pretending."

I smiled slightly. "That feels like a gentle no."

She smiled back. "It's just timing."

"I respect that."

She nodded once, satisfied.

"Have a good day, Elijah."

"You too."

And then she was gone - not rushing, not lingering, just continuing on with her life.

I stood there longer than I needed to holding on to the moment.

On the walk home, I realized I was smiling - not because I'd gained something, but because I hadn't pushed for it. The moment felt clean. Unforced. Unfinished in a way that didn't irritate me.

Later that afternoon, I did something I hadn't planned.

I walked into a store I passed all the time and never entered.

A puzzle shop.

I walked the aisles, scanning shelves filled with images meant to come together piece by piece. Landscapes. Maps. Skylines. Art reproductions.

Then one caught my eye.

A city at dusk. Warm light. Depth without chaos. Familiar, breath-taking but safe.

I bought it without overthinking.

At home, I went into the room I rarely used — the one with the table, the one that held the evidence of what I never finished. I didn't organize the pieces. Didn't sort by color or edge.

I opened the box and scattered them.

All of them.

Across the table. Across the floor. Across the order I usually needed.

Ten thousand pieces.

Then I sat down.

Picked up one edge.

Then another.

I started where I always did - the outside.

Not because I knew where it was going.

But because, for the first time in a long while, I wanted to see.

I glanced at the box again, back at all the pieces and thought…

Maya.

Small Cafe

I didn't see Maya again for a while, but the memory of our encounter returned more often than I expected. Not in a way that interrupted my work, but in the moments between things - the elevator ride up to my office, the stillness of my penthouse at night, the moment just before sleep when the world settles and the mind begins to wander.

It wasn't obsession.

It was more like an awareness that something in the air around me had shifted.

One Friday afternoon, I stopped at a small café near my building, a place I rarely visited but for some reason felt drawn to. I ordered an espresso, chose a seat by the window, and opened my laptop. I wasn't working on anything important. I was just sitting there, letting the low hum of conversation and the soft clatter of cups give shape to the silence.

Halfway through my drink, I felt movement near the entrance.

I turned and to my surprise Maya walked in, sunlight catching the soft coils of her hair, a small dog trotting beside her in a harness like he owned the place.

I blinked once, slow and almost amused by the timing.

She spotted an open seat and started toward it - then stopped.

Her eyes met mine.

A slow smile spread across her face. Not surprised. Not startled.

Just pleased.

"Well," she said as she walked over, "if I didn't know better, I'd think you were following me."

I gestured toward my laptop. "I could say the same."

She laughed softly. "Please. If I were following you, I'd at least pretend to be subtle."

The dog tugged her toward my table with determined enthusiasm. I bent down and scratched behind his ear.

"You must be Bruno."

She smiled. "Yes, this is my furry best friend. Bruno, this is Elijah."

Bruno barked once.

"You two go everywhere together?"

"Yes. He has separation anxiety."

Bruno barked again.

"See?" she added dryly. "He agrees."

I nodded toward the empty chair. "Sit with me."

She hesitated for a moment, as if out of habit she was looking for a reason not to - but then she smiled, set her cup down, and eased into the chair. Bruno curled up at her feet.

She sat back calmly. "So… tell me something."

"Like what?"

"Anything. I just want to hear you talk."

I wasn't sure whether to laugh or ask why. Instead, I answered honestly.

"I'm not used to being asked that."

"Well, get used to it," she said. "I like knowing people. Not their accomplishments. Them."

I took a breath. "Alright. I like mornings better than nights."

"Why?"

"They're simple. Honest."

She studied me for a moment. "I can see that. You feel like a morning."

"A morning?"

"Yes. Collected. Focused. A little quiet until the light comes in."

I raised an eyebrow. "You pay attention."

"I do," she said. "You'd be surprised how many people don't."

She leaned forward slightly. "Now tell me something about me."

I pretended to consider it. "You named your dog after someone tough with a bad attitude."

She gasped. "Bruno is a saint."

I glanced down at him licking the floor. "He seems very holy."

She laughed - a soft, easy sound that did something unexpected in my chest.

"Alright," she said. "Now something real."

I smiled. "You said one more."

"I know," she said, her eyes bright. "Last one."

I paused, then said, "I don't talk to many people like this."

"Like what?"

"Open. Without thinking about it."

Her expression softened. "That's interesting."

"It's surprising."

"Well," she said gently, "you carry a lot."

She wasn't wrong.

We talked for nearly an hour about nothing and everything. Small things. Random things. Teasing. Laughing. Letting silence sit between us without rushing to fill it.

Eventually, she checked the time.

"I should go," she said. "Bruno has therapy."

I frowned. "Therapy?"

"Oh yes," she said seriously. "He has issues."

Bruno barked.

"Denial," she added.

I stood as she gathered her things. "Tell him good luck."

She smiled. "This was nice."

"It was."

She hesitated, then said, "I'm free Sunday afternoon. If you're interested."

"In what?"

"Coming to church with me."

I wasn't expecting that.

But I wasn't resisting it either.

"What time?"

"Twelve."

"I'll be there."

She smiled and scribbled her number on a napkin.

As she walked away, Bruno trotting proudly beside her, I stared at the napkin in my hand.

Church.

That wasn't what I expected, neither was her number.

But something in me knew that if I wanted to know her, I'd have to go where she was.

She was worth it.

And somehow I knew this was the beginning of something.

I just didn't know what.

Church

Sunday morning came earlier than I expected.

I woke before my alarm, lying in the soft gray quiet of my penthouse, staring at the ceiling as if the day had something waiting for me I couldn't yet name. I wasn't nervous. I wasn't resistant.

I was simply excited to see her again.

I showered, dressed in something simple but presentable, and paused in front of the mirror longer than usual. I couldn't remember what people wore to church anymore. My mother used to put me in stiff shirts with polished shoes and full suits.

That morning, I chose clean button-down and dark slacks. Nothing loud or trying to say more than I was ready to say.

When I stepped outside, the air already held the promise of warmth.

I stood for a moment on the sidewalk, unsure which direction to go - feeling faintly ridiculous about how long it had been since I'd walked into a church on purpose.

I checked the address again on my phone.

Seven blocks east.

The walk felt longer than it was.

Not because of distance, but because of the strange awareness that I was walking toward something that didn't belong to my usual rhythm.

I saw her before she saw me.

She stood near the front steps of the building, her hair pulled back loosely, sunlight catching the edges of her face. She wasn't scanning the street. Wasn't checking her phone. Wasn't waiting in any anxious way.

She was simply there.

When she noticed me, her expression softened into a smile that felt more like recognition than greeting.

"Good morning," she said.

"Morning."

"You found it."

"I did."

She nodded, like that mattered.

Bruno wasn't with her.

"I left him home," she said. "He once barked during communion."

I smirked. "Sounds about right."

"He thinks the wafers are a snack."

I laughed quietly.

She looked pleased by that.

"Ready?" she asked.

"Yeah."

She turned and started up the steps.

I followed.

The church was larger than I expected, but not overwhelming. Warm brick. Tall windows. People arriving with a kind of relaxed familiarity.

The moment I stepped inside, something shifted. Not dramatically. Not spiritually. Just a soft awareness of atmosphere.

Families greeting each other. Older women hugging younger ones. Children running toward volunteers. Laughter folding into piano chords drifting from somewhere inside.

Maya watched me take it in.

"You good?" she asked.

"Yeah," I said. "Just… observing."

She nodded. "Don't overthink it. Just be."

The sanctuary was bright. Sunlight filtered through stained glass in soft colors that touched everything gently. The music was full but not loud. Sincere, not performative.

Maya stood beside me, raising her hands slightly, swaying with the rhythm.

I stayed still.

But something in me opened.

Not wide. Just enough to let the warmth in.

The pastor spoke about identity. About the difference between who we are and who we learned to be in order to survive. About the walls we built from childhood that become our protection as adults.

About how God wasn't looking for perfection.

Just willingness.

The words landed precisely.

They felt like they knew my name.

My hands were clasped loosely in front of me. My eyes stayed forward. A strange tension settled in my chest.

Not pain.

Not comfort.

Recognition.

Maya glanced at me once, only to be sure I wasn't overwhelmed. Then she looked back toward the front.

She didn't guide me.

Didn't interpret.

Didn't rescue me from anything.

She just stood beside me.

Like that was enough.

After the service people lingered. Conversations bloomed easily.

Maya introduced me to a few friends.

"This is Elijah," she said. "A friend."

The word settled into me in a way I hadn't expected.

As we walked back toward the car, she looked at me with quiet curiosity.

"What did you think?"

I exhaled slowly. "It was… different."

"Good different?"

I nodded. "Yeah. Good."

She smiled, not triumphant, not proud. Just pleased.

"I'm glad you came."

She offered to drive me home, I was glad she did just to have a few more moments with her.

On the drive back we talked about ordinary things. Music. Food. Bruno's ongoing vendetta against the mailman.

I didn't realize how much I was smiling until she noticed.

"Look at you," she said. "Grinning like someone told you a secret."

"Maybe someone did."

Her eyes softened. "I hope it was something good."

When the car stopped outside my building, neither of us moved right away.

"Thank you," I said finally. "For today."

"You're welcome. And hey, no pressure. If you never come again, I won't guilt-trip you."

She paused.

"Well. Maybe gently."

I laughed. "I might come back."

Her head tilted. "Yeah?"

"Yeah," I said. "I liked being there."

She nodded. "Then that's enough for today."

I stepped out. The door closed. The car pulled away.

Inside my penthouse the space felt different.

Not heavy. Not empty. Just… wider than I was used to noticing.

I set my keys on the counter, slipped off my shoes, and walked a few steps in when my phone rang.

Marcus.

I answered it without thinking much of it.

"What's up."

"Man, I just got off the phone with Cynthia. Remember her from our frat days?" he asked.

"How can I forget, loud and proud Cyndi. What's happening?" I replied.

"She just asked about you." he responded.

I leaned against the counter. "That's random."

"Right," he said. "So, what you been up to today."

I hesitated.

Then I said it.

"I went to church."

There was a pause.

Then a loud -

"You did what."

I almost laughed. "Relax."

"No, no. You. At church?"

"Yeah."

"It must be a woman."

"I didn't say that."

He exhaled through a grin I could hear. "You didn't have to."

I shook my head slowly. "We're just getting to know each other."

"That's how it starts."

"Bro."

"Hey, I'm not judging. I'm impressed." he said.

"For going to church?" I asked.

"For letting someone in."

That made me pause.

"Sound like she's good for you," he added more carefully.

"You don't know her." I said.

"I know you."

I didn't respond.

"Man," he went on, "enjoy it. Whatever it is. Let it be good while it's good."

I stared across the room, at nothing particularly.

"I'll talk to you later." I said.

"Don't forget about my party next month." he said.

"I'll be there"

"Cool, later." The line went dead.

I stood there for a moment, then found myself walking down the hallway toward the puzzle room without really deciding to.

I stopped in the doorway.

I didn't move.
I didn't touch anything.

I just stood there with the echo of the message from church in me, the warmth of Maya beside me still lingering, and a deep realization that I was changing.

Cracked Doors

I woke earlier than usual the next morning, long before the sun stretched across the city skyline. For a while, I didn't move. I lay there staring at the ceiling, thinking about Maya's softness, the quiet way her face had lit up when I showed up at church.

I had to admit, it had felt right.

Eventually I got up, showered, dressed, and made coffee I barely tasted. My phone sat on the counter, face up, already carrying a weight of expectation.

It buzzed before I reached for it.

Emily: *Morning trouble.*

A photo followed. Bare shoulder. Morning light. That familiar half-smile that always carried invitation with it.

Emily: *You've disappeared on me.*

I exhaled slowly.

Me: *Long days.*

Three dots appeared instantly.

Emily: *Liar. But I forgive you.*

Emily: *When are you coming over?*

I stared at the screen longer than I needed to. There was a time when I would've already been reaching for my keys. A time when that question felt like oxygen.

Me: *Not sure. Busy.*

Emily: *Busy doing what?*

Me: *Working.*

A laughing emoji.

Emily: *You work too much. Come over and let me fix that.*

That was her gift. Her danger.

She didn't ask me to open. She asked me to forget. She didn't invite me into her world. She pulled me out of mine.

And God help me - it always worked.

I didn't respond right away. I picked up my mug, took a sip, set it down untouched.

Me: *Maybe later.*

Enough to keep the door open. Not enough to walk through it.

Another notification appeared.

Maya: *Good morning.*

Maya: *Bruno says hi.*

A picture followed. Bruno wrapped in a blanket like a burrito, eyes half-open and deeply offended by the day.

I smiled before I realized it.

Me: *He looks like he needs deliverance.*

Maya: *He will absolutely get some next Sunday.*

Me: *Funny. You have plans today?*

Maya: *Work. And then a walk later. You?*

My eyes drifted down the hallway toward the closed door of the puzzle room.

Me: *Nothing planned.*

Maya: *Okie doke.*

Me: *You want to meet later?*

A few minutes passed.

Maya: *Sure.*

One word. No seduction. No pull. Just presence.

And somehow that felt more dangerous.

Later that afternoon we met at the café. Maya looked effortless in a way that couldn't be taught. Soft colors. Relaxed presence that felt like breath instead of fire. Bruno wore a ridiculous bandana that read I AM THE MOMENT.

"Really?" I asked.

She shrugged. "He chose it."

Bruno barked once in agreement.

She carried that same faint citrus warmth I remembered from the first night. Simple. Natural. Unforced.

We talked easily. Nothing rehearsed. Nothing strategic. Just conversation arriving as it came.

At one point, she studied me quietly.

"Have you ever been in love?" she asked.

I looked away before I answered.

"No."

She nodded like that made sense.

"You feel like someone who's always been close," she said. "Close enough to connection that it hurts. Not close enough to trust it."

She wasn't accusing me. She wasn't diagnosing me. She was just noticing.

My phone buzzed on the table.

Emily: *You seem like you're ignoring me. That's new.*

I didn't answer.

Maya noticed the vibration. She didn't comment on it. That somehow made it louder.

That night, back in my penthouse, the quiet felt charged in a way I wasn't used to.

Emily: *Come over.*

Emily: *I miss your hands.*

The words were familiar. Effective. Stirred something in me, just not in the place that felt like choice anymore.

Me: *Another night.*

Emily: *You're different lately.*

She was right.

I stood by the window looking out over the city, thousands of lives unfolding beneath me, and felt the truth settle in without drama.

Emily was momentum. Maya was gravity.

Emily lit me up. Maya slowed me down.

Emily made me feel powerful. Maya made me feel seen.

Emily asked me to escape. Maya asked me to stay.

Those were not the same thing.

And for the first time, I wasn't sure I wanted fire.

I wasn't sure I wanted distraction.

I wasn't sure I wanted intensity if it cost me depth.

I didn't close the door on Emily.

But I stopped standing in the doorway.

And that felt like the beginning of a decision I wasn't ready to name yet.

Old Rhythms

Thursday arrived with the kind of light that softened the city. The sky was clean, the air mild, and even the sidewalks seemed less impatient. I finished a meeting earlier than expected and checked my watch.

Three hours until I saw Maya.

I tried to focus on emails, but my thoughts kept drifting toward her. The way she laughed. The way she said my name. The quiet weight she left behind after I walked away from her. It wasn't distraction. It was orientation. Like my internal compass had shifted slightly and hadn't recalibrated yet.

I shut my laptop and stood, stretching.

Nadia leaned into my doorway. "You heading out?"

"In a bit," I said. "Just taking a minute."

She smiled. "Big plans tonight?"

I considered downplaying it, then didn't. "Yeah."

"Good," she said. "You work too much. You need a life that isn't on a calendar."

"You schedule my life," I replied.

"Exactly," she said, and walked off.

I was gathering my things when Emily appeared in my doorway.

"Hey, stranger," she said, leaning against the frame. "You hiding from me or just too important now?"

"Just busy," I said.

"Aren't we all," she replied. "You got a minute?"

I checked the time. I did.

"Sure."

She stepped inside, closing the door with easy familiarity. "I've got two tickets to that rooftop jazz thing downtown. Tonight. Eight o'clock. You like jazz?"

I did. But the idea of canceling on Maya tightened something in my chest.

"I already have plans," I said.

"Reschedule," she smiled. "Live a little."

"I can't."

She studied me, then softened. "Are you seeing someone?"

The pause answered before I did.

"That sounded like a hesitant maybe," she teased.

"It's complicated."

She smiled like she'd won something. "Well, until it's not, the offer stands."

She reached the door, then glanced back. "I'm not going anywhere."

I watched her leave with something uneasy settling in me. I knew how this worked. Attraction, proximity, opportunity. Lines blur quietly and then all at once.

I pulled out my phone.

Me: *See you at seven.*

Maya replied almost instantly.

Maya: *I'll be ready. Bruno will be judging.*

I smiled despite myself.

Later, I pulled up outside her building. She came out in a soft dress and light jacket, hair flowing, face fresh. Bruno trotted beside her like a chaperone with opinions.

"Well hello, gentleman," she smiled.

"Evening," I said. "Hi, Bruno."

He sniffed my shoes and gave a small approving huff.

Music played low as we drove.

"How was your day?" she asked.

"Meetings about meetings," I said. "You?"

"Client calls, community planning, and a woman who tried to donate a broken couch and call it generosity."

I laughed. "How'd that go?"

"I thanked her," she said. "Then prayed she never comes back."

Dinner was warm and tucked away. Candlelight. Soft music. Wood and low voices. The kind of place that made you slow down without trying.

We talked. About childhoods. About mothers. About disappointments. About small joys.

"You ever think about reaching out to him again?" she asked.

My father.

"No."

"Why not?"

"I don't chase what already told me it doesn't want to be caught."

She watched me quietly. "That little boy might disagree."

"He doesn't get a vote anymore."

"Maybe he should."

She didn't press.

On the ride back she rested her head against the seat. "I like being around you."

"Why?"

"You're present," she said. "Even when you're guarded."

When we reached her door, she turned toward me.

"Thank you for tonight."

"I like you," I said.

"I know."

We stood close. The night leaned in around us. I stepped forward. She didn't move.

Her phone lit up.

She glanced at it. "Work stuff."

"I should go," she said.

She paused at the door. "I enjoyed tonight."

"So, did I."

She went inside.

My phone buzzed.

Emily: *Rooftop was amazing. You missed out.*

I stared at the text too long.

The essence of Maya rode with me the entire ride home. I could think of only her. Emily messaged again, I didn't respond.

I told myself - lines only blur when you let them.

What was budding with Maya, I was not willing to chance.

Blurred Lines

The week moved forward in its usual shape.

Same meetings. Same hours. Same rhythm.

But I didn't move with it the same way.

I texted Maya most mornings. Not to fill space, but because I wanted the day to start where she was. Her replies were easy. Light. Observant. Something about Bruno's moods, something she overheard, or some small moment that made her smile. She never pressed and only offered peace.

I liked that about her.

Monday morning, I walked into the office and found Emily leaning against my doorframe, coffee in her hand.

She was… stunning. That was the truth of it. Long lines, warm skin, curves that suggested softness even when she was sharp. Her perfume reached me before she did. Something expensive. Something designed to linger.

Any other week, we would've explored a long lunch.

I hated that I noticed that.

"You disappeared this weekend," she said.

"I was busy."

She smiled, unoffended. "You always are."

She handed me the coffee. Black. No sugar.

She knew what I liked.

"Thank you."

She stayed where she was, watching me.

"You seem… somewhere else lately."

"Tired," I said.

She tilted her head. "You've been tired before."

I didn't respond.

"You should let me take care of that." she said gently.

"Emily…"

"I know. Complicated."

She smiled like it didn't scare her.

"But complicated things end all the time."

I met her eyes and said flatly. "I need to get back to work."

She didn't hesitate. "Let's go to lunch."

Right then, I was at a crossroads. Maya would never know, plus we aren't together. Yet, something inside me knows that if I do this, I would hurt her….us. Can't take that chance.

"I'm seeing someone."

Her eyebrow lifted. "Are you dating her?"

I didn't answer.

"Are you exclusive?"

Silence.

She nodded slowly. "Then you're not seeing someone. You're getting to know someone."

That word stayed with me longer than the conversation did.

My desk phone rung, perfect timing.

"I have to take this, client." I said while reaching toward the receiver.

"I'll see you around." She turned and walked slowly out of my office.

****

Later in the week, Maya called while walking Bruno.

Her voice always has a way of softening the edges of my day.

I smiled without trying.

It was our night to meet but a client emergency kept me later than anticipated.

Me: *Running late. I'll explain later.*

Maya: *No problem. Be safe.*

I hoped she meant it.

By the time I stepped outside, the city had shifted into night. Lights on. Noise softer.

And there was Emily.

Standing near the valet.

Perfectly composed.

"You look wrecked," she said.

"I need to go."

"I'll walk with you."

"No need."

But she fell into step beside me anyway.

"I really wish you would talk to me." she said quietly. "Did I do something?"

"You've done nothing." I said.

"Then what is it, some girl you've just met. How do you even…

I stopped her mid-sentence. "Emily."

She stopped too.

"If you're not with her, you don't owe her fidelity."

"I've had a long day and I'm headed home."

Before she could respond –

A bark cut through the air.

Loud. Bright. Familiar.

My stomach dropped.

Across the street, Maya stood with Bruno.

Still.

Watching.

Her eyes moved from me to Emily.

Emily straightened beside me. "Is that her?"

Maya crossed the street calmly. No rush. No emotion.

She stopped in front of me.

"Elijah."

Her voice wasn't sharp.

It was soft.

"I can explain."

She smiled gently. "You don't need to."

Emily folded her arms. "So you're the maybe-girlfriend."

Maya's gaze stayed steady. "No, I'm Maya, I can assure you I'm not anyone's maybe."

She looked at me once more.

"Take care of yourself."

Then she turned.

"Come on, Bruno."

And she walked away.

Something in my chest went hollow.

Emily turned to me. "That's her? Oh please, she could never satisfy your appetite. I know you."

I looked at her.

"Emily," I said quietly. "We're done."

Her face shifted.

"What?"

"We are done."

She stared at me, disbelief turning into something wounded. "You don't get to do what you want with me and walk away like I'm just another notch on your belt," she said. "Like I didn't matter."

I turned toward the valet.

"Elijah," she called, her voice sharp. Then softer. "Wait."

I kept walking.

"I'm in love with you."

I stopped.

But I didn't turn around.

I didn't say anything.

The valet placed the keys in my hand. I thanked him, got into the car, and closed the door.

For a moment, I looked at her through the windshield.

Then I pulled away.

I called Maya.

No answer.

I drove past her place. The light was on. I slowed, then parked across the street, sitting there longer than I meant to.

I didn't want to show up unannounced.
Didn't want to intrude on whatever she might be thinking.
Didn't want to make things heavier than they already were.

Eventually, I drove home.

Inside my penthouse, the silence felt different.

Not empty.

Exposed.

For the first time in years, I spoke into the quiet.

"God… if you're real… show me what to do."

And that was all I had.

Pulled Back

Maya didn't block my number.

She didn't fire off a sharp message or demand explanations I didn't yet know how to articulate. She didn't accuse me, didn't corner me, didn't try to win clarity by force.

She simply withdrew.

And I understood, too late, that this was how she held her boundaries. Cleanly. Without spectacle. Without needing permission or agreement from the person on the other side of them.

This was what it looked like when she closed a door.

That night, I lay flat on my back staring at the ceiling, the phone resting on my chest like it carried a gravity of its own. The room was dark, but not truly dark. The city leaked in through the windows, a muted glow bouncing off glass and steel and distant movement. Somewhere below, traffic hummed. Somewhere else, people laughed. Life continued at a pace that felt offensive in its normalcy.

Every few minutes, I lifted the phone.

Nothing.

No missed calls.
No notifications.
No soft concern disguised as casual conversation.
No "Are you okay?"
No "We should talk."

Just absence.

Silence, when chosen, is not empty. It is full. Heavy. Intentional.

I typed a message.

Maya, please call me.

Deleted.

Typed again.

I need to talk to you.

Deleted.

Typed again.

I'm sorry. Please let me explain.

My thumb hovered over send, trembling with urgency, with fear, with the need to collapse the distance she had created. I turned the phone face-down instead.

I didn't trust myself not to fill the space with language that sounded like justification. And I didn't want to be that man. The one who talked instead of told the truth. The one who flooded silence because he couldn't sit in it.

I didn't sleep.

At some point after sunrise, exhaustion blurred into something fragile. I sent a message anyway.

Me: *Maya, I'm sorry about last night.*

No reply.

An hour later.

Me: *It wasn't what it looked like.*

Still nothing.

Three hours after that.

Me: *I care about you. Please don't shut me out.*

Each message felt like a knock on a door that would not open. Each unanswered line echoed louder than the last.

By evening, my body had given up, but my mind hadn't. I paced the penthouse without direction, opening the refrigerator only to stare at its contents, closing it again untouched. I poured a drink and left it sweating on the counter, forgotten. The quiet felt amplified, pressing against my ears, my ribs, my thoughts.

What replayed itself relentlessly wasn't confrontation.

It was her face.

Not anger.
Not accusation.
Just that stillness behind her eyes.

The kind that doesn't argue.
The kind that doesn't bargain.
The kind that decides.

That was worse than fury.

She wasn't punishing me. She wasn't trying to make me feel small. She simply refused to live inside confusion. And the respect I felt for that sat painfully beside the fear that she might never let me back into clarity.

The next morning, I went to work like someone stepping into weather without shelter. Nadia took one look at me and didn't tease like she usually did.

"You good?" she asked.

"Yeah," I lied without thinking.

She tilted her head, studying me. "You look like you fought a ghost and lost."

I huffed a breath that almost passed for a laugh. "That's… unsettlingly accurate."

Emily showed up near noon.

She always announced herself before she spoke. Today was no different. A silk blouse the color of ivory caught the light as she stepped into the doorway, smooth and deliberate, paired with a sleek maroon pencil skirt that fit like intention. Every line of her was polished. Controlled. Purposeful.

The way she commanded rooms without effort seemed almost calculated.

But not this time.

I didn't soften when I saw her. Didn't lean back. Didn't create space the way I used to. I stayed exactly where I was, grounded in my chair, eyes steady, body still.

"Not today, Emily" I said before she could speak.

The words landed between us, clean and unmistakable.

She paused, just slightly. A flicker passed over her face - surprise, maybe, or recalibration. Then she lifted her hands in a small, disarming gesture.

"Relax," she said. "I came to apologize."

That stopped me.

"For what?" I asked.

"For pushing," she said. "For assuming. For crossing lines, I shouldn't have crossed."

I searched her face, unsure how to receive something I hadn't expected.

"I didn't know she was serious to you," she added.

I exhaled slowly.

Emily nodded once, accepting the shift. "Well. I wish you the best."

She left without ceremony.

The rest of the day passed in a haze of practiced competence. I had always been good at compartmentalizing. But that night, the penthouse felt louder in its quiet than it ever had before.

Without realizing it, I walked into the puzzle room.

The boxes sat where they always had. Stacked. Ordered. Dozens of beginnings. Dozens of things I had never finished. I lowered myself to the floor and pulled out the puzzle I had started, the one I had imagined completing with Maya beside me. The bottom row and side perimeter intact. The rest waited.

I sifted through thousands of pieces with restless hands.

Nothing fit.

Frustration surged, sharp and sudden. I shoved the box away, stood abruptly, grabbed my phone, and pressed her name.

It rang once.
Twice.
Three times.

Then voicemail.

Her voice filled the line. Familiar. Warm. Steady.

"Hey, you've reached Maya. Leave a message."

My throat tightened.

"Maya," I said quietly, "I know you don't want to talk to me right now. I know what it looked like. But you're not casual to me. You're not just someone I talk to."

I paused, grounding myself.

"I don't want complications. I don't want anyone else. I want you. And I'm sorry it looked otherwise."

Silence.

"Please call me back."

I ended the call feeling more exposed than I had in years.

The next day passed without reply.

The day after that too.

On the third day, her name appeared on my screen.

My breath caught. My body went still.

I answered immediately.

"Maya?"

"Hey."

Her voice was calm. Gentle. Not guarded, but not open either.

"I didn't call to revisit the past," she said. "I just didn't want to leave things in silence."

"Does that mean…"

"It means I'm listening," she said quickly.

Relief washed through me so hard it almost knocked me off balance.

"I didn't lie to you," I said.

"I know," she replied. "That's not why I stepped back."

"Why then?"

"Because I didn't like how I felt," she said simply. "I don't chase confusion. It's not healthy for me."

I nodded, even though she couldn't see me.

"I miss talking to you," I admitted.

"I miss talking to you too."

"Can we meet?" The words came quickly, I couldn't miss the chance.

She hesitated.

"Tomorrow. After work."

"Anywhere." I said before she could reason out of it.

"My place is fine," she said.

"Yes. I'll be there."

"Good night, Elijah."

"Good night, Maya," my heart smiled as the call ended.

I stood at the window, my reflection barely visible against the city lights, studying the man looking back at me. The one who had finally understood the cost of carelessness. The one who knew what was at stake now.

"Don't mess this up, Eli," I murmured.

Right then, I realized I was willing to do whatever it took to make this right.

And for the first time, I trusted myself to mean it.

Lesson Learned

I arrived at Maya's building ten minutes early but stayed in the car, hands gripping the steering wheel as if the leather could steady my thoughts. I wasn't nervous about seeing her. I was afraid of mishandling whatever she offered when she opened the door.

I rehearsed nothing. I didn't want a speech. I wanted honesty, the kind I wasn't always comfortable giving because it required surrender instead of control.

At exactly six, I took a breath, grabbed the small bag of food I'd picked up on the way, and headed inside. The elevator rose too fast, too slow, I couldn't tell. My heart beat a little harder the closer I got to her floor.

I knocked once.

The door opened.

There she was.

Standing in soft clothes, hair loosely tied, face calm. She wasn't guarded, but she wasn't wide open either. Her expression held something measured, something thoughtful. Something that said she had things she needed to hear, and things she needed me to understand.

"Hi," she said.

"Hi," she stepped aside. "Come in."

I entered quietly, Bruno walking up to me with a softer bark than usual, sniffing my shoes before trotting back to his bed. Even the dog seemed aware of the weight in the room.

"I brought dinner," I said, holding up the bag.

"Thank you." She motioned to the small dining table. "We can sit."

We moved around each other carefully, politely, like two people attempting to rebuild something without cracking it.

She opened the bag with our dinner, no pleasantries like usual. Asked which entree was mine, then gently placed it in front of me with silverware. She did the same for herself and sat down.

We ate a few bites in silence.

Finally, Maya gently set down her fork.

"Elijah."

I looked up.

She waited a beat. "I want to hear what happened. Not the polished version. The real one."

I nodded slowly. "Okay."

I took a breath. "Emily works at a marketing firm in my building. She's… persistent. I should've handled it better. I should've stopped her sooner. I should've made boundaries clear before it looked like there were none."

Maya held my gaze. "And why didn't you?"

The question wasn't sharp. Just honest.

"Because I'm used to keeping people at a distance," I said quietly. "Letting things stay casual. Staying in control. I didn't think it mattered… until you."

She folded her hands on the table.

"When I saw you two together," she said, "I didn't think you were lying to me."

I exhaled. "Then what did you think?"

"I thought you were undecided," she said. "And I don't do indecision. Not because I'm hard. Because I've done that before. I promised myself I wouldn't do it again."

That landed in my chest.

"You didn't deserve that moment," I said. "Or the confusion."

"You're right, I didn't," she agreed softly.

I met her eyes. "I'm sorry, Maya. Truly."

She let the apology reach her.

"I believe you," she said.

Relief flickered through me.

"But belief isn't the same as trust."

"I know."

She stood and walked toward the window. I followed with my eyes, the quiet strength of her presence grounding the room.

"I need clarity, Elijah," she said. "It's what keeps me steady. I need to know where you stand… with me."

I rose and stepped closer, not touching yet.

"I stand," I said, "in a place I haven't stood my entire life. Somewhere I didn't expect to find. With someone I didn't expect to meet."

She turned to face me.

"I think about you more than I want to admit," I continued. "I look forward to you. I feel something new when I'm with you. And I'd like to build on that."

"So what do you want, Elijah?"

I stepped closer.

"You," I said.

Her breath shifted.

She hesitated, then said quietly, "When I saw you with her, I didn't know what to think."

I stayed still.

"It felt like I walked into something unfinished."

I reached for her hand then, gently, intentionally, wrapping my fingers around hers.

"I'm sorry," I said again, softer this time. "She was never a relationship. We just kept each other's company. But she was never my present nor my future."

Her shoulders eased.

"I understand," she said.

Bruno barked once, as if approving.

She met my eyes again. "If we're doing this," she added, "we do it honestly. Clearly. No blurred lines."

"I want that."

"Good," she said. "Because I'm not into playing games."

"I won't do that to you."

"Then we'll take this slowly," she said. "Together."

I nodded.

The space between us thinned, not with urgency, but with intention.

I leaned in slightly and kissed her forehead.

I wanted her to believe in me…needed her to.

We moved to the couch afterward, her head against my shoulder, my arm around her, nothing else needed.

And for the first time, I knew the difference between comfort and connection. This was connection.

And it was real.

New Rhythms

The week after we reconciled at her apartment felt different than anything I was used to.

Nothing dramatic happened but there was a quiet shift I could feel under my skin, in the way my shoulders relaxed when her name lit up my phone, in the way my day felt slightly off if I went too long without hearing her voice.

It wasn't a loud change. It didn't announce itself. It didn't demand attention. It simply existed, like a new rhythm my body was slowly learning to move to.

We didn't see each other every day. Neither of us needed that. We still texted in our normal, light rhythm.

Maya: *Good morning. Bruno says today is optional.*
Me: *Tell him rent is not.*
Maya: *Rude. He's reporting you to HR.*

Those small exchanges became anchors in my day. Proof that she was there. Proof that I was there. Proof that whatever we were building didn't need constant tending to stay alive.

Some nights we talked on the phone. Some nights we didn't. When we did, the conversations were a mixture of teasing and depth, of surface jokes and questions that reached further than either of us pretended to be ready for.

One evening, I called her while looking out over the city, the view that usually made me feel detached. That night, it just felt far away.

"What are you doing?" I asked.

"Cooking," she said. "Trying not to burn dinner."

"Do you know what you're doing?"

"That's irrelevant," she replied. "What about you?"

"Thinking."

"That sounds heavy," she said. "Do you want company in your head or distraction?"

I paused. "Both."

"I can do that."

We stayed on the line while she cooked, while I walked from window to couch to kitchen to nowhere in particular. We weren't always talking. Sometimes I just listened to the sound of her moving around, stirring something, humming off-key to whatever song was playing.

I realized I liked the sound of her life moving alongside mine.

On Sunday, I went back to church with her.

I didn't overthink it this time. I just went. I sat next to her, sang a little under my breath, listened more than I meant to. During worship, she slipped her hand into mine. She didn't look at me when she did it. She just held on.

I didn't pull away.

I didn't even consider it.

After service, an older woman stopped us with a knowing smile. "It's good to see you here again, young man."

"It's good to be here," I said.

Maya glanced up at me, warmth flickering in her eyes, like she was quietly proud of something I hadn't realized I'd done.

As we walked to the car, she asked, "What did you think of today?"

"It felt different."

"How?"

"Less like something I was visiting," I said, "and more like something that might actually fit."

She didn't push it. She just nodded and squeezed my hand.

"That's enough for now," she said.

And somehow, it was.

We grabbed lunch afterward. Nothing fancy. We shared fries, laughed too loud, argued about pineapple on pizza, and spent ten solid minutes debating whose group chat was more chaotic.

Somewhere between the laughter and the empty basket of fries, I realized I was looking at her differently. Not like someone I was spending time with, but like someone who had quietly stepped into a space in me I hadn't known was empty.

She caught me staring.

"What?" she asked, smiling.

"Nothing."

"Don't do that," she said. "If you're going to look at me like that, at least say something."

I thought about it for a moment.

"You feel like home and an interruption at the same time," I said.

She blinked. "That's a powerful sentence for a Sunday."

"It's true."

"Then I'll take it."

Her voice softened when she said it, like she understood more than she was saying.

After that, life settled into a gentle rhythm. Work. Small pockets of time together. Walks in the park where Bruno dragged us in wide, unnecessary circles. Quiet evenings that didn't need plans.

One afternoon she brought lunch to my office. Nadia watched the exchange with a look I chose to ignore.

Later, Nadia said, "You look lighter."

"Do I?"

"Like your shoulders finally realized they don't have to carry everything."

The comment stayed with me longer than I wanted to admit.

Nadia had always seen more than most people did.

A few nights later, we sat on Maya's couch. Candles flickered. Bruno slept upside down, completely unbothered by the world. A movie played in the background that neither of us was really watching.

She turned toward me.

"Do you ever think about the future?" she asked.

"In what way?"

"In the way that matters."

I stared ahead for a moment before answering.

"I watched what I thought was a perfect life fall apart because of one decision. Honestly, the future doesn't excite me. It haunts me. I'm afraid I'll end up like him."

She didn't hesitate.

"Elijah, you're not your father," she said gently. "You don't run when things get real. You stay. You face things. You're stronger than you think. That's why I'm giving this a chance."

The weight of her words settled between us.

"Thank you," I said quietly. "I won't disappear."

She held my gaze. "If you ever do, I won't chase you."

"I know."

And I did know. That was what made her different. She wasn't asking me to stay out of fear or need.

She was asking me to stay by choice.

Then she told me about the trip.

"I'll be out of town for three weeks," she said.

The words came out before I could stop them.

"What? When do you leave?"

"Next week," She said.

"Your job just dropped that on you?"

She gave a small, understanding smile.

I already knew the answer.

It came with the territory.

That didn't make it any easier to hear.

"Not really," she said. "It's been in the air for a few months. But the client has an immediate need. Duty calls."

I nodded, taking that in.

"I'll miss you," I said.

She tilted her head slightly. "You will?"

"Yes."

Her expression softened. "I'll miss you too."

There was no drama in the moment. No heaviness. Just honesty resting quietly between us.

Later that night, after I kissed her forehead and drove home, I found myself walking to the puzzle room.

I sat down at the table, facing the unfinished scene.

For a while, I just looked at it. Then I picked up a piece. And another.

I didn't sort by color.
I didn't start with the edges.

That wasn't how I usually worked.

This time, my hands weren't steady. My thoughts weren't quiet. Airports kept crossing my mind. Distance. Absence. The unfamiliar tension that comes when you finally care about something enough to feel the risk of losing it.

I held one piece longer than necessary.

"I'll finish this when you come back," I said quietly.

The words felt like a promise.

And for the first time, I wasn't just building the borders of something.

I was preparing for the part that required patience.

The part that required trust.

The part that meant working through the middle.

Slow Return

The morning Maya left felt heavier than I expected.

I woke before my alarm, the city still wrapped in that pale, early light that makes everything look softer than it truly is. I dressed quietly, grabbed coffee I barely sipped, and drove to her apartment in a silence that clung to the edges of my thoughts.

I told myself it was only a few weeks. I told myself distance didn't mean forever.

None of it sounded convincing.

When she opened the door, suitcase beside her, she looked exactly like herself. But her eyes carried that familiar mixture of excitement and something gentler, something like sadness wearing a brave smile.

"Good morning," she said.

"Morning."

She stepped back to let me in. Bruno rushed to me immediately, tail wagging slow and low, the kind of wag that meant worry.

I knelt and ran a hand down the dog's back. "You taking care of your mom?"

Bruno barked once, offended at the implication he ever did anything less.

Maya laughed softly. "He's been dramatic all morning."

I stood. "Can't imagine where he gets it from."

"I'm offended." She said, jokingly nudging my arm.

She checked the time. "We should head out."

I grabbed her suitcase. She grabbed Bruno's leash, even though she wasn't taking him, like she needed the comfort of holding it one last time. At the car, she knelt down and kissed Bruno's head.

"Be good for Auntie Keisha," she whispered. "And don't tear up her shoes. That's mean."

Bruno whined as if promising nothing.

We drove in a silence, the kind that comes when a moment means more than either person has the vocabulary to express.

Maya looked out the window at the passing buildings. "Thank you for driving me."

"You don't have to thank me," I said. "I wanted to."

She smiled faintly. "I know. That's why it matters."

I glanced at her, then back at the road. "You nervous?"

"A little," she admitted. "But it's a good nervous. Growth nervous."

I nodded slowly. "I'm proud of you."

She turned toward me, eyes softening. "That means more than you know."

I reached for her hand, kissed it and held it the rest of our drive. I didn't want to let her go.

When we reached the airport entrance, I parked, grabbed her suitcase, and walked with her inside. The terminal was busy, with echoing conversations, rolling luggage, families hugging, couples saying goodbye. The kind of atmosphere that made everything feel temporary and important at the same time.

At the security line, she turned to me, folding her arms lightly across her chest.

"So," she said, "this is the part where I act composed even though I'm not."

"You don't have to act."

She smiled. "But I want to. It's my thing."

I stepped a little closer. "You'll be fine, Maya."

"Can I be honest," she said.

"Of course," I said.

"It's not work, I just… don't like leaving something that feels good."

"You're not leaving it," I said.

"You sure?"

"Yes," I answered. "We're not losing anything. It's three weeks. We'll talk. We'll call. We'll live normal."

She let that settle. I could see her deciding to believe me.

"Elijah," she said softly, "don't close off while I'm gone. Don't slip into your own world. I don't want to come back to a man who's retreated."

"I won't," I said.

She looked at me for a long time, reading me with the part of herself that understood people deeper than their words. Whatever she saw seemed to ease something in her.

"Okay," she whispered.

A boarding call echoed across the terminal. She lifted her suitcase handle and took a breath.

"Well. This is me."

I nodded. "This is you."

She leaned in and hugged me, not a polite hug, not a careful one, but something warm and sure and full. I held her gently, breathing in the scent of her hair, the curve of her shoulder, the small tremor of her breath.

For a moment, the entire airport disappeared.

When she stepped back, she held my gaze.

"I'll miss you," she said.

I didn't hide it. "I'll miss you, too. More than you know."

She started toward the boarding line, hesitated, then turned back.

"Elijah?"

"Yeah?"

"Don't disappear."

I nodded once. "I'm here."

She gave me one last look, soft, full, trusting, and then she turned and walked toward the gate.

I watched her until she was out of sight. Watched until the last glimpse of her slipped behind the corner. Watched until there was nothing left to watch.

Only then did I exhale.

I walked back to my car, each step echoing louder than the last. I sat behind the wheel for a moment, hands resting loosely, staring at the steering wheel as if expecting it to offer guidance.

I waited for the feeling to fade.

It didn't.

I drove home slowly, replaying her smile, the squeeze of her hand, the look she gave me before turning away.

And when I stepped inside my penthouse, I went immediately to the puzzle room.

Opened the door.

Stood in the center of the room, staring at the unfinished puzzle on the table.

I walked toward it and rested a hand on the edge.

"I won't disappear," I said quietly, as if reminding myself.

But the silence of the room didn't answer back.

And when I turned off the light and walked out, something small but significant shifted inside me.

Not a storm.
Not a collapse.

Just a tremor.

A tiny crack in an old, familiar wall.

The beginning of something loosening.

The beginning of the unraveling I didn't yet see.

Back Again

The first three days without Maya passed quietly.

I filled them the only way I knew how, with work. Meetings folded into more meetings, and the evenings stretched deliberately into late nights until the line between day and night barely registered.

Busyness had always been my shield. It kept me moving fast enough to stay ahead of the hollow places, the spaces where something might surface if I slowed down long enough to notice it.

But absence has a way of making itself known.

Even in silence.

It wasn't loud or demanded attention. It lived in small spaces. In the empty chair across from me at lunch. In the silence of my apartment when I instinctively reached for my phone to hear her voice. In the extra minute I stood in the kitchen at night, holding a glass of water I didn't even want.

My rhythm began to shift. Some mornings I woke up too early and couldn't fall back asleep. The next, I overslept.

My body felt slightly out of sync, as if something it had grown used to was no longer there. My routine, once precise, now felt slightly misaligned. Not broken. Just missing something.

We still texted every morning.

Me: *Good morning.*

Maya: *Good morning. I am alive. Barely. They have us hiking and smiling at once. Pray for me.*

I smiled at my phone longer than I meant to. Sent back a half smile emoji, which was the most honest I allowed myself to be.

She sent pictures from hotel rooms that all looked the same. Neutral walls. White linens. A suitcase half unpacked. She sent photos of her team at dinner, faces flushed from long days and shared jokes. She called me one night and described a ridiculous training exercise they had her doing, laughing so hard she could barely finish the story.

I sent pictures of my coffee mug. My desk, my favorite pen. The cuff links or tie I decided to wear.

I didn't send pictures of the quiet, never made mention of the torture I felt.

In the evenings, we talked. Sometimes for twenty minutes. Sometimes just long enough to hear each other breathe.

"How was your day?" she asked one night.

"Fine," I said. "Busy."

"What kind of busy?"

I hesitated. "The usual."

My answers stayed short. Not intentionally. It was just easier. Familiar. A way of being that had protected me for years. Details had a way of opening places I wasn't trying to face.

She noticed.

"You okay?" she asked gently.

"Yeah," I said. "Just tired."

"From what?"

I stared at the wall across from me. "Everything."

There was a pause on the line. Not heavy. Not accusing. Just present.

She let it pass.

That was the thing about Maya. She never forced her way in. She waited at the door and trusted me to open it.

But waiting only works if someone actually moves.

We ended each call softly. No tension or pressure. Just warmth held carefully between us.

"Talk tomorrow?" she asked.

"Yeah," I said. "Tomorrow."

When the line disconnected, the penthouse felt more like a distant island than my home.

On the fifth night, I wandered into the puzzle room without turning on the light. The moonlight filtered in faintly through the window, just enough to outline the table in the center of the room.

The unfinished puzzle waited for me.

I stepped closer, fingertips hovering over a piece before pulling back as if it might sting. I had never been afraid of unfinished things before. Only of finishing them and realizing nothing had changed.

"Stay steady," I whispered to the quiet. "Do not drift."

The room did not answer and I didn't touch a piece that night.

The next day crushed me slowly.

A meeting stretched longer than planned. Expectations rose, numbers refused to bend and voices ran hot. By the time I left the office, my temples throbbed and my shoulders felt carved from stone.

I checked my phone in the elevator.

A message from Maya.

Maya: *Call me if you need me. I am here.*

I stared at it.

Did not reply.

Not because I didn't want to. But because exhaustion and old instincts tangled together and silence felt easier than explaining myself.

I told myself I would respond when I got home. After a shower. After food. After the weight in my chest loosened.

I told myself a lot of things.

When I stepped into the penthouse, I dropped my keys on the counter and leaned forward, palms flat against the marble. The surface was cold beneath my skin.

"Just get some sleep," I muttered.

I did not sleep.

I sat in the dark, whisky in hand, staring at the outline of furniture I knew by heart.

My phone lay face down beside me like an accusation.

And I ignored it.

That was the truth of it.

I ignored her.

All of sudden, the doorbell rang.

The sound cut through the silence like glass.

I looked toward the door, confused. No one came here unannounced.

I opened it slowly.

Emily stood in the hallway.

Her eyes were red, breath uneven. Her hair looked as though she had run her hands through it one too many times.

"Elijah," she said, voice trembling. "Can I come in?"

My chest tightened.

"What's wrong with you?" I asked flatly.

I should've closed the door.

Instead, I hesitated.

That was all it took.

She stepped closer than was comfortable. "I needed to talk to someone. You said if I ever needed anything, I could reach out."

"That was months ago," I said carefully while folding my arms. "And you should not be here."

"I know," she said quickly. "I just had a horrible argument and I didn't know where else to go."

She moved forward again.

I stepped back.

"Emily." I said firmly, "This is inappropriate. Do not ever…."

She interrupted me softly. "Just a minute. I promise."

I hesitated.

That hesitation would echo later.

"Fine," I said. "A minute."

She entered, wiping her face, gratitude flooding her expression as if kindness itself had invited something deeper.

She sat on the edge of the couch, shoulders curled inward.

"I hate being alone," she whispered.

I remained near the doorway, arms crossed. "What does that have to do with me."

She looked up, eyes searching my face for something I could not give.

My phone vibrated on the counter.

I knew before I looked - Maya.

I walked over and checked the message.

Maya: *Just checking on you. Haven't heard back.*

Something inside me dropped.

Not slowly.

Not gently.

It gave way all at once.

The room felt smaller. The air felt thinner. Emily was still talking, her words drifting around me like background noise, but I barely heard them.

Because in that moment, the truth hit me with brutal clarity.

I had let silence do my talking.

I had let distance grow comfortable.

I had convinced myself that avoidance was the same as handling things.

And Maya, the woman I cared about, had just sent me a message filled with concern while another woman sat on my couch.

Emily followed my gaze. "You okay?"

No. I wasn't. And I knew it.

The guilt wasn't dramatic. It didn't flare or demand attention. It settled deep in my chest…heavy, making it hard to breathe.

I imagined Maya in that hotel room, checking her phone and wondering why I hadn't answered.

I imagined her brushing it off. Telling herself I was busy. Telling herself not to overthink.

And I hated that I had put her in that position at all.

Emily said my name again.

"Elijah?"

I turned to her slowly and she moved right in front of me. Then she reached out, resting her hand against my chest - not pressing, not grabbing. Just there. Enough to feel my heartbeat. Enough to feel my body react before my mind could stop it.

I closed my eyes briefly, jaw tightening.

Any other night. Any other week. I would've slid into the familiar and I can't lie, my body wanted her.

But Maya's face rose in my mind uninvited. The way she trusted me. She didn't hand that out casually.

I opened my eyes.

"Emily," I said firmly, stepping back. "This stops here."

She frowned. "You're aroused," she said quietly, not accusatory. Observant. "Don't pretend you're not."

"I didn't say I wasn't," I replied. "I said this stops now."

The distinction mattered.

She searched my face, trying to find the crack, the weakness she'd learned to exploit. When she didn't find it, frustration flickered across her expression.

"So what," she scoffed. "You're just going to suddenly be a good man?"

I met her gaze, steady. "I'm going to be an honest one and you need to leave."

Her face shifted. "What?"

"Leave," I said. "Right now."

She stood, confusion and hurt crossing her expression. "I just needed…"

"This isn't your place to need from," I cut in, firmer now. "Not anymore."

She looked at me like she didn't recognize me.

"You've changed," she said.

"Good," I answered.

She grabbed her purse, pride rising to cover the sting. "You don't get to treat me like I'm nothing."

"I'm not," I said. "What we had is over., it's the past. Please do not come here unannounced again."

She stood there a second more, composed her blouse as the distressed damsel act miraculously disappeared. Without another word, she walked out.

When it shut behind her, the apartment fell silent again.

But this time, the silence felt different.

This time it had a shape.

I stood there for a long time.

My phone was still sitting on the counter.

Maya's message glowed on the screen.

Maya: *Call me if you need me.*

I stared at it.

I did need her.

But if I called now, what would I say? That Emily had just been there? Would I tell the truth? Would I soften it? Would I lie? And what if Emily came back while I was on the phone?

I wasn't ready to explain this yet.

I told myself, to be safe…just call tomorrow.

She Knows

I didn't sleep.

I lay on my back staring at the ceiling, the city moving faintly outside the window, my body exhausted but wired, my mind replaying everything I wished I could erase. Emily's perfume still lingered in the air, faint but unmistakable. I hated that more than anything. I'd opened the windows twice. It didn't matter.

I hadn't crossed the line.

But I sure stood close enough to see it.

To feel it.

To know exactly how easy it would have been to fall.

That was the part I couldn't shake.

Not the almost. The uncontrollable *desire.*

The moment where my body responded before my conscience did. Where instinct surged up like an old, primalistic current that I couldn't shut it down fast enough.

I had seen it in her eyes the second she noticed. The flicker of satisfaction. The knowledge that she still had access to something in me I'd sworn I was done giving away.

But the damage was already done, I shouldn't have opened the door.

I rolled onto my side and grabbed my phone from the nightstand.

No new messages.

Maya didn't text anymore that evening.

That alone wouldn't have rattled me before. She wasn't clingy. She had a full life. She didn't hover. That was one of the things I respected about her.

But this silence felt different.

Heavy.

Earned.

I scrolled up, rereading the last message she'd sent me the night before. Just checking on you. Haven't heard back.

I'd stared at it for a long time.

Too long.

I told myself I'd reply after I settled down. After I figured out how to explain the tension in my chest without sounding like a man making excuses. I told myself I didn't want to worry her while she was away.

The truth was simpler.

I didn't want to hear disappointment in her voice.

Because disappointment meant I mattered enough to lose.

I set the phone back down and ran a hand over my face. My jaw ached from clenching it. My body felt wrong, like it was carrying a charge with nowhere to go.

I got up and went to the room where my past failures lingered.

The light remained off. I didn't need it.

A faint light shined through the shutters just enough to show me the table. The puzzle sat there unfinished, pieces scattered in careful disarray. The one I'd told myself I would finish when she came back.

I dropped into the chair and stared at it.

This was what I did when things got complicated. I controlled what I could. Edges. Order. Progress that didn't require emotional risk.

But tonight, even the puzzle felt like it was watching me.

I picked up a piece, turned it over in my fingers.

My hands weren't steady.

I set it back down.

Maya would have noticed that. The way my voice shifted when I lied by omission. The way I pulled inward instead of outward. She would have felt the absence before I ever admitted it.

She always did.

That was what scared me.

I checked my phone again.

Nothing.

A familiar urge rose in my chest. The instinct to retreat. To let silence stretch until it turned into distance. To convince myself that if something fell apart quietly, it wasn't really my fault.

I hated that instinct.

I hated that it still lived in me.

By morning, my nerves were shot. I showered, dressed, went through the motions of a man who looked composed from the outside and fractured from the inside. At the office, people talked. Numbers moved. Decisions were made. I nodded. I answered questions. I smiled when expected.

But everything felt muted.

Around noon, I finally called her.

It rang twice before going to voicemail.

I didn't hang up.

"Hey," I said when the tone sounded, my voice lower than usual. "It's me. I just… I wanted to hear your voice. Call me when you can."

I stared at the phone after I ended the call, willing it to buzz.

It didn't.

That afternoon dragged. Each hour without a response felt heavier than the last. By the time I left the office, my chest felt tight, my thoughts looping in a way I couldn't control.

I drove home without turning on the radio.

When I stepped into the house, the silence felt intentional. Like it was waiting for me to say something honest.

I didn't.

I dropped my keys, loosened my tie, and stood in the middle of the living room, unsure what to do with my own hands.

This was the part no one talked about.

Not temptation.

After.

The guilt that didn't scream but pressed. The clarity that came too late. The realization that doing the right thing didn't erase the fact that you almost didn't.

I hadn't betrayed Maya with my body.

But I had come closer than I wanted to admit.

And somehow, that felt worse.

My phone buzzed just as I sat down.

A text.

Maya: *Finished early. Back in Dallas Friday.*

No emoji. No warmth. No softness.

My stomach dropped.

I read it again.

And again.

I typed quickly.

Me: *I'll send a car for you.*

Her reply came almost immediately.

Maya: *No need. I'll arrange a ride.*

The distance in that sentence was unmistakable.

Me: *Maya... please let me pick you up.*

This time, the pause stretched longer.

Then -
Maya: *No need.*

I set the phone down slowly.

For the first time, panic cut through the fog.

Not the dramatic kind.

The kind that comes when you realize someone is intentionally moving into an invisible reality.

I leaned forward, elbows on my knees, staring at the floor.

This was the cost of unfinished work.

Of wounds I'd managed instead of healed.

Of discipline without understanding.

Maya wasn't punishing me.

She was protecting herself.

And the worst part was, she now needed to protect herself from me.

I closed my eyes and exhaled through my nose as if the breath would lift the heaviness in my chest - it didn't.

If she walked away, it wouldn't be because she didn't care.

It would be because I hadn't learned how to show up correctly.

And that truth sat with me, heavy and unmovable, as the evening settled in and the city lights blinked on one by one.

For the first time, I didn't reach for distraction. No whiskey, no night caps, no television or scrolling.

I just sat there, staring at the walls, in the void, feeling every ounce of it.

Knowing, deep down, that whatever came next, was at my own expense.

Gone Cold

I didn't plan to stop the car.

That's the truth of it.

I was driving with no destination, letting the streets carry me the way they had for years - forward, always forward, never asking why. The lights from the city blurred past the windshield, my hands gripping the wheel like it was the only thing keeping me upright.

My phone sat in the console, face down.

No new messages.

No Maya.

The silence felt accusatory now, like it knew something about me I didn't want to admit.

That was when I saw it.

A church.

Old, brown brick, non-descriptive. The kind of building that looked like it had stood through more storms than it advertised. No glowing signs. No flashing screens. Just a small white placard near the sidewalk.

Thursday Night Service

There were maybe eight cars in the lot.

I drove past it.

Then slowed.

Then stopped at the light.

My chest tightened for no reason I could explain. A pressure built behind my sternum, familiar and unfamiliar all at once. The kind of feeling I used to outrun. The kind I'd trained myself to ignore.

"Don't," I muttered to myself, exhaling hard.

But my hands turned the wheel anyway.

I pulled into the lot and parked crooked, not bothering to straighten the car. I sat there with the engine running, staring at the brick wall ahead of me as if it might speak first.

My breath grew shallow.

The pressure intensified.

And then, without warning, my face crumpled.

Not in a dramatic way. Not sobbing. Just… collapsing inward.

"Lord," I said aloud, my voice cracking against the quiet of the car, "I don't know how to do this."

The words surprised me.

They didn't sound polished. They didn't sound strong.

"I don't know what to do," I continued, forehead dropping against the steering wheel. "Why would you leave me alone with no one?"

My hands shook.

"Please," I whispered, the word barely making it out. "Help me."

I sat there until my breathing steadied, until the engine heat crept up my legs and reminded me I was still alive. Then I turned the car off and stepped out into the cool night air.

The church door opened with a soft groan, as if to announce my arrival.

Inside, the space was dim and simple. Wooden pews worn smooth from decades of bodies sitting in the same places, carrying the same burdens. The walls held old hymn boards and framed scripture that had yellowed with time. There was no spectacle here. No performance.

Just presence.

I slid into a pew near the back, shoulders squared out of habit, even though no one was watching. I didn't bring a Bible. I hadn't owned one in years.

But there was one waiting for me in the rack in front of the seat.

I picked it up slowly, my fingers brushing the thin, crumpled pages like they recognized something before my mind did.

The service moved quietly. A few songs. A piano that wasn't perfect but felt honest. Then the pastor stepped forward.

She was a woman.

That startled me.

Not because I doubted her authority - but because I wasn't expecting the familiarity of a woman's voice to meet me here.

She didn't pace. She didn't raise her voice. She stood steady, hands resting at her sides, eyes scanning the room like she could see straight through every defense we'd brought with us.

And then she said it.

"There are people in this room," she said calmly, "who have built their entire lives on control."

My spine stiffened.

"People who learned early that survival meant composure. That strength meant control. That if you could just hold it together long enough, no one would see how much it hurt."

My chest tightened.

"You were praised for it," she continued. "Called responsible. Called dependable. Called strong."

The word *strong* landed like a blow.

"But survival is not healing," she said. "And control is not character."

My breath caught.

"Some of you didn't cross the line," she went on, "but you stood close enough to feel the heat. Close enough to recognize yourself in the reflection and not like what you saw."

My hands curled into fists.

"And God is not asking you to manage yourself better," she said. "He's asking you to lay yourself down."

The tears came fast then. I tried to swallow them. Tried to straighten up. Tried to do what I'd always done.

It didn't work.

As the piano began to play and she lifted her hands, inviting anyone who was tired of carrying themselves to come forward, I didn't think.

I stood.

My legs moved before my pride could stop them.

I walked down the aisle with my head bowed, tears spilling freely now, my chest heaving like I'd been holding my breath for years and just realized it. When I reached the altar, I dropped to my knees hard enough to feel it in my bones.

The floor was unforgiving.

My hands braced against the carpet, my breath uneven, my body shaking with something deeper than sadness. This wasn't about one mistake. Or one woman. Or one bad night.

This was about years.

Years of holding myself together with discipline and distance. Years of confusing restraint with strength. Years of standing close to the edge and calling it control.

I felt it then - an ache so deep it almost knocked the air from my lungs.

And in that ache suddenly I wasn't there anymore.

I was standing in a hospital room, the hum of machines filling the air.

My mother's hand in mine.

Her skin thin. Her voice steady.

"Elijah," she said gently, the way she always did when I rushed myself, "don't rush your process."

The memory hit me so hard I gasped.

I remembered how she said it when I wanted to grow up too fast. When I tried to be the man of the house before I was ready. When I thought strength meant never breaking.

Her voice echoed again, softer now, "missing pieces doesn't mean the picture is ruined."

I realized at that moment, I never cried at her funeral. I hadn't let myself feel her.

Not really.

Until now.

My shoulders collapsed inward as a sob tore out of me, raw and unguarded. I pressed my forehead to the floor, my hands curling into fists as years of unspoken grief finally found a way out.

I didn't notice when someone knelt beside me.

But then a hand rested gently on my back.

Not heavy. Not forceful.

Steady.

"You don't have to hold yourself together here," the pastor said softly.

Her voice was close now, grounded, real.

She didn't rush me. Didn't try to stop the tears. She just stayed, her presence calm and sure, as if she had seen this before and wasn't afraid of it.

After a moment, she spoke again.

"I sense, you learned early how to survive." she said quietly, "You learned how to function. How to lead. How to endure and often alone. But Jesus didn't come so you could endure life alone. He came to give you something better, something new."

I sucked in a shaky breath.

"Not improved," she continued. "Not managed. New, it's called salvation."

The word echoed through me.

"You don't have to earn it," she said. "You don't have to prove anything. It's not some reward you get when you finally get it right. It's a gift for finally admitting you can't do it by yourself."

I lifted my head slightly, my vision still blurred.

She met my eyes.

"If you're ready," she said, "you can give Him everything you've been carrying. The fear. The control. The shame. The grief. He paid the cost so you don't have to."

My voice came out hoarse. "I don't know how."

She smiled softly. "That's okay. I'll help you."

She didn't make it dramatic. Didn't raise her voice. Just spoke slowly, clearly, inviting me into each word.

"Jesus," she said gently, "I need You. I believe You are who You say You are. I ask You to come into my heart. I confess my sins and ask for your forgiveness. Make me new. I give You my life right now."

The words trembled as I repeated them.

But they were mine.

When it was done, she placed her hand over my clasped hands and prayed.

At that moment something moved inside me and she must've felt it because as it moved, she reassured me. "You're not alone anymore," she said. "And you don't have to become someone else overnight. Just stay honest and willing."

I stayed kneeling there for a long while after that.

Not empty.

Held.

When I finally stood, my legs felt weak, my chest lighter, my breathing slower. Something fundamental had shifted. Not everything was fixed. Not everything was clear.

But I was no longer carrying myself.

That night, back home, I knelt beside my bed and prayed. Not out of desperation this time. It was instinctive.

"Maya comes home tomorrow," I whispered. "God, let Your will be done."

For the first time in a long time, sleep came easily.

Deep. Restful.

And whatever waited for me in the morning, I knew this:

I was not the same man who had walked into that church.

And even if Maya never chose me again -

I had finally chosen truth.

Everything Changed

I slept better than I had in years.

Not the kind of sleep that comes from exhaustion, but the kind that settles deep into your bones when something heavy has finally been set down. I didn't dream. I didn't toss. I didn't wake with my jaw clenched or my mind racing through problems.

When I opened my eyes, the light in the room felt serene. Less demanding. I lay there for a while, staring at the ceiling, breathing slowly, almost like I was learning how to do it again.

Nothing in my life had magically resolved. Maya was still gone. The damage I had caused was still real.

But something inside me was quieter.

Not fixed.

Just steadied.

Before I could overthink it, I called into work.

I hadn't done that in seven years.

The words felt unfamiliar coming out of my mouth. "I won't be in today." No explanation. No justification. Just a decision. I supposed I had earned the day, but it still felt strange to claim it.

Outside my window, the city looked pale and undecided, softer than I had ever noticed. I stayed in bed a few minutes longer, letting the unfamiliar calm settle instead of questioning it.

Maya was coming home today.

The thought didn't crash into me the way it might have a week ago. I didn't rehearse conversations. I didn't imagine outcomes. I knew better now. Whatever was going to happen between us wouldn't be won by strategy or control. It would happen because it was real or it wouldn't happen at all.

I moved through the morning slowly. Showered without rushing. Let the water hit my shoulders longer than usual. Made coffee and actually tasted it.

By the time I drove to the airport, my hands were steady on the wheel. My chest still tight, but not frantic. I wasn't rehearsing speeches. I wasn't plotting outcomes. I was simply present in the waiting.

I stood at her gate, hands in my pockets, watching passengers spill out in clusters. Families. Couples. Strangers reuniting like nothing had ever gone wrong between them.

Then I saw her.

She emerged from the crowd with her carry-on rolling behind her, shoulders squared, quick paced, face tired but composed. Her hair was pulled back, effortlessly gorgeous.

She looked down at her phone and then up toward the cars parked, scanned the area and then saw me.

Our eyes locked. She didn't smile.

My heart really started pounding, as if to remind me of what was at stake.

She walked toward me and stopped just short, leaving space between us that felt deliberate.

"Elijah," she said, her voice calm but distant.

"Maya. I'm glad you're back."

"I can't," she said immediately. "I've had a long flight, and I don't need whatever this is."

Her words weren't cruel. They were clean. Final in a way that didn't invite negotiation.

"Please," I said quietly. "Let me take you home."

"I already paid for a ride."

"I'll cover it."

She studied my face, exhaustion and resistance warring behind her eyes. Finally, she nodded once, tight and reluctant.

"Fine."

I walked to the driver, thanked him, handed him the cash. Took her bags myself. She didn't thank me. She didn't look at me. And I didn't expect her to.

The drive was quiet.

Not the kind of silence that buzzes with tension. The kind that settles, heavy and unresolved. I didn't rush to fill it. Didn't reach for explanations she hadn't asked for. I knew better than to mistake urgency for honesty.

"Would you like something to eat?" I asked once, my voice even.

"No."

We drove on.

A few paces before her building, I slowed and pulled over instead of pulling directly up. The decision surprised even me, but something in my chest insisted this couldn't be said casually, parked like some convenience.

Turning toward her, I said finally. "I need to tell you something."

Her eyes flicked toward me, then back to the windshield. "Okay."

I took a deep breath.

She reached for the door again. This time, I gently took her hand.

"Maya," I said quietly.

She exhaled slowly. "Go ahead."

"When you left," I began, "I didn't handle it well. Not because of you. Because I didn't know how to sit with what I was feeling. I've been alone a long time. Longer than I admitted."

Her posture stiffened, but she didn't interrupt.

"Emily came to my place. It was unannounced and she was hysterical." I said. The words burned on the way out.

"I didn't shut it down the way I should have, I let her in."

Her head snapped toward me. "You did what?"

"I didn't sleep with…"

She snapped, turning toward me sharply, her face hardened.

"So when I leave for work," she said, voice sharp now, "I'm supposed to worry that your separation anxiety will drive you into another woman's arms?"

"No, you don't." I said.

"Elijah," she continued, eyes flashing, "I am not a Goodwill and I'm not a dump. I am not the place you leave your mess and expect me to sort through it."

"I'm not asking you to do that," I said.

"You already did," she replied. "And I won't."

She got out of the car before I could say anything more.

I exhaled, turned the engine off, and got out calmly, opened the trunk and grabbed her luggage quickly yet gently, like this was something I knew how to do.

She was seething.

I handed her the suitcase. I handed her the suitcase. She snatched it from my grip.

"Maya, please…"

"No," she said. " I'm not interested in managing your unresolved wounds. I am done."

The words landed clean and final.

She turned and walked toward the building, each step sharp, decisive.

I stood there, watching her go.

I didn't chase her. I didn't ask her to understand.

I watched until the door closed behind her and the glass reflected only my own stillness back at me.

Then I went back to the car and sat down, my hands resting loosely in my lap.

This was the cost, the consequence.

She was gone.

I bowed my head and spoke quietly into the silence, not bargaining, not asking for anything in return.

"God… I love her." My voice caught in my throat, slightly.

"Don't take her away too. But if You have to…I know it's your will. Just let love find her.

I sat there for a while, letting the weight of it settle.

Then I started the car and drove away.

Moving On - Maya

I was sitting idly on the sofa when I realized how much of him had followed me home.

Elijah showed up everywhere in my life. In the small, quiet things like the indentation on the cushion beside me where we both enjoyed a movie together once, we laughed so hard I cried that night. The expression on his face was priceless.

Everything reminded me of him, even the faint hum of the city outside carried the wind of his voice, like a new rhythm and it refused to forget it.

Bruno lay curled against my legs, his warmth was comforting as I rested my hand on his back, fingers moving absently through his brown fluffy fur. His slow and steady breathing, grounded me in the one thing in the room that wasn't painfully complicated.

Everything looked the same.

But I wasn't.

That unsettled me more than I wanted to admit.

I hadn't planned to think about Elijah tonight or every night since the first hello. I told myself I was past it, past the questions, past the moment at the airport – he looked so handsome when I walked out that airport. As angry as I was, I wanted to run into him arms and kiss him.

He was such a beautiful man. The kind you notice before you mean to.

Tall, with a build that carried strength without trying to prove it. His shoulders were broad, his chest firm beneath whatever he wore, and his arms… defined in a way that made you aware of them without staring too long. There was control in them. Not just power, but restraint. The kind that made you wonder what it would feel like to be held by someone who knew exactly how much strength to use.

Everything about him was clean. Intentional. Even the way his clothes rested against him felt deliberate, like they belonged there. Nothing excessive. Nothing out of place. Just… right.

And then there was his scent.

Warm. Subtle. Inticing.

The kind that drew you in without asking. It didn't reach for you, didn't overwhelm. It stayed low, quiet, and somehow that made it more noticeable. It lingered in a way that made distance feel temporary – it was now resting in my pillows.

Up close, he was even harder to resist.

There was something in the way he carried himself, steady, grounded, unmoved.

And that was the danger of him.

He didn't try to be anything more.

He didn't have to.

And somehow…he had my full attention.

It was hard to be mad with him, but I was.

Every thought of him lodged itself somewhere deep and stubborn inside my chest. I managed to work my way to the weekends, but stillness has a way of pulling truths to the surface. It doesn't rush you. It just waits until you're quiet enough to hear.

And tonight, I felt the pain.

I couldn't deny it.

I leaned back into the couch and stared at the ceiling, letting my thoughts drift despite myself. The way he listened when I spoke. The way his voice softened when he said my name, like it was something he handled carefully. The way his silence that night had felt heavier than any argument ever could.

That was the part that kept circling back.

Not the presence of another woman. Not even the possibility of betrayal.

The absence.

The unanswered call.
The delay.
The space where reassurance should have been.

My chest tightened just slightly.

I told myself I was being dramatic. That grown women don't spiral over a call not being answered. That life happens. Work happens. Distance happens. But I had learned the hard way that sometimes silence isn't neutral. Sometimes it's a language all its own.

And I spoke it fluently.

I shifted slightly on the couch and let out a slow breath, feeling the weight of it settle somewhere greater than I was prepared for.

I liked him.

Not casually. Not in passing. Not in a way that could be dismissed or redirected when it became inconvenient.

I liked him in a way that rearranged things.

In a way that caught me off guard, shifting something internal I had grown used to keeping still. There was a quiet peace in it, something steady and grounding, but beneath that… something else. Something unpredictable. Something that felt like it had the power to change more than I was ready to offer.

And that was the part I couldn't ignore; it was unnerving.

Because peace had never felt this close to risk before.

And that scared me.

I wasn't sure when it happened - when liking him stopped being a pleasant possibility and started becoming something else entirely. The affection started asking more of me than I'd planned to give.

Do I love him? I thought. The fact that I had to ask myself the question at all felt… revelatory.

Bruno stirred, lifting his head to look at me, as if checking in.

"I know," I murmured, rubbing behind his ear. "I don't like this either."

I stood and walked into the kitchen, the movement deliberate, like I was trying to shake something loose. This time I reached for the wine instead of the tea. The sound of the glass filling felt real. Present. Honest.

"I'm not doing this," I said aloud, leaning against the counter, as if to convince myself.

Emily's name surfaced again, uninvited and irritating.

I shook my head. "I'm not fighting a door that should already be closed. How dare he waste my time."

Bruno padded in behind me, sat, and looked unimpressed.

Back on the couch, the ache was even thicker now, more insistent. The kind that presses questions against your ribs until you acknowledge them.

Then my phone buzzed.

Once.

I glanced down, expecting a work email.

Instead, his name lit up the screen.

And three words.

Elijah: *I'm sorry, Maya.*

It caught me totally off guard.

I stared at the message, reading it repeatedly. Not because I didn't believe it. But because I didn't know where to place it inside me.

I set the phone down slowly.

I needed clarity before I spoke.

So, I closed my eyes and whispered a prayer so faintly it barely existed outside my own chest.

"Lord… help me discern what's real."

Bruno sighed dramatically at my feet, and despite everything, I smiled.

I picked the phone up again and typed.

Then deleted it.

Typed something else.

Deleted that too.

Finally, I wrote what felt honest without being reckless.

Me: *We need to talk. Not tonight. Tomorrow, after church. Your place.*

I hit send before I could talk myself out of it.

The phone felt heavier in my hand afterward.

I leaned back into the couch, wine untouched on the table, heart steady but alert. Whatever this was - whatever Elijah was becoming, whatever I was beginning to feel - it deserved truth.

Even if truth led somewhere painful.

Even if it led away.

Bruno shifted closer, warm and grounding.

And for the first time that evening, I didn't rush past the feeling or try to tame it.

I sat with it.

The knowing settled in first, followed by the ache, then the quiet weight of possibility.

But I knew something in me had changed.

And pretending otherwise would have only been me lying to myself.

Grace in the Middle

Across the city, late afternoon light slipped between the buildings as I drove home from the gym, the windows cracked just enough to let the cool air wash over me. My body was exhausted in the right way - worked, stretched, spent. Not the restless exhaustion I'd lived in for years, but something cleaner. Something earned.

I felt wrung out. Emptied. Cleared.

The drive didn't rush me the way it usually did. My mind was clear. No replaying conversations or rehearsing apologies. Just steady and calm. The kind of calm that doesn't demand anything from you.

When I reached the penthouse, I didn't turn on music. Didn't check my phone. I walked through the living room, the echo of my footsteps familiar but no longer heavy. In the kitchen, I poured a glass of water and drank it slowly, deliberately, like a man who wasn't running from his own thoughts anymore.

There was nowhere else I needed to be.

I picked up my phone, stared at it for a moment longer than necessary, then typed the words that had been sitting in my chest for weeks.

Me*: I'm sorry, Maya.*

Nothing more. No explanation. No defense. No reaching. Just the truth, offered without conditions.

I set the phone down and sat on the couch. Reached for the remote. Stopped.

Instead, I picked up the Bible.

It was new - too new. Thick, heavy, expensive in a way that felt intentional. Full-grain leather, deep oxblood brown, the pages edged in gold, red-letter text catching the light. It felt substantial in my hands. Like something meant to last.

I hadn't grown up with a Bible like this. Ours had been thin, soft-spined, passed between hands until the cover peeled. This one felt chosen.

I opened it without a plan.

Genesis first. Beginnings. God speaking things into existence when there was nothing but darkness and water. Then Matthew - genealogies, names stacked on names, proof that legacy mattered even when people forgot it did. John came next. Slower. Deeper. Words that didn't rush me. *In the beginning was the Word.* Something about that settled in my chest.

Later, 1 Corinthians. Love, discipline, order. Then Philippians - joy written from a prison cell. That one stayed with me, too. Joy that didn't depend on circumstances. Joy that survived loss.

The days that followed took on a strange rhythm. I read between meetings at work. Early mornings before the city woke up. I rushed home not to escape - but to sit with the Word open in my lap. It steadied me in the growing realization that Maya might never come back to me.

And somehow, that didn't undo me.

My puzzle room - the room I'd avoided for weeks - no longer felt like a threat. It didn't call out to me with accusation. It waited.

That evening, I walked in.

The sun from earlier had faded, replaced by the soft amber glow of the lamp in the corner. The unfinished puzzle sat on the table exactly where I'd left it. *Maya.* Skyline pieces scattered. Edges somewhat built. Middle incomplete.

For the first time, I didn't feel dread looking at it. No fear that I was about to repeat myself again.

I felt… ready.

I pulled out the chair and sat down. Picked up a piece. Ran my thumb along its edge. It wasn't the final piece. It didn't hold anything together. It was just blue and silver - sky, maybe water.

It fit.

I placed it gently, then set aside the pieces that didn't. No forcing. No frustration. Just trust that what didn't belong yet would, eventually.

"Faith," I murmured aloud, the word tasting new and old at the same time.

Faith is the substance of things hoped for, the evidence of things unseen.

I exhaled slowly. "God… I don't believe it's over. You said all I have to do is ask. So here I am. Asking."

The thought came suddenly - clear, insistent.

Aunt Toni.

I hadn't called her in years. I sent her money every month, yes. A text around holidays but voice-to-voice? No. And yet my hand was already lifting the phone.

It rang twice.

"Elijah?" Her voice cracked open something in me instantly.

"Hey, Aunt Toni."

"Oh, baby," she said, emotion thickening her words. "I've been praying hard for you. I didn't know why - I just knew you needed it."

I closed my eyes, relief spreading through me like warmth. She was in her eighties now, but her spirit was still sharp. Still anchored.

"You good, son?" she asked gently. "I haven't heard from you in a long while."

"I apologize for that." I said. "Your voice sounds just like Moms and it was… hard to talk to you." That was the truth, I normally gave excuses via text.

"Oh, sweetheart," she whispered. "I know. I know. Thank you for taking care of me. I just kept praying for you anyhow."

"I'll do better," I promised. "I gave my life to Christ, Aunt Toni." There was a bit of silence. Then -

"Ohhhhh my Lord!" she cried. "Praise God! I *knew* it. I knew it was a reason you were in my spirit. Tell me everything."

Her excitement was warming, I told her about the church, the pastor and alter. Not every detail. Just the bones of it. Then I shared about Emily showing up. Maya's hurt. My fear. My cowardice.

She didn't interrupt. Didn't gasp. Didn't correct.

"Well," she said finally, "God can reconcile anything."

"I want to fix it," I admitted. "All of it."

"You can't fix it," she corrected softly. "But you can show up. You can be different. And you can let God finish what you've been trying to build by yourself."

Her words settled in me - not as rebuke, but as release.

"When you talk to her," she continued, "don't tell her you've changed. Show her. And don't ask her to heal wounds you haven't handed to God yet."

I nodded even though she couldn't see me. "I think I'm finally ready to hand them over."

"Good," she said, smiling through the phone. "Then let God lead. I see the change already."

"Thank you." I said relieved.

"Always, baby. Always. Let me pray for you."

She prayed - and it felt like she stepped inside my chest, swept the corners and dusted the remaining residue I didn't realize was still there.

When the call ended, I sat there for a long time.

Lighter. Not free from consequence. Not untouched by loss.

Just liberated.

"Where the Spirit of the Lord is, there's liberty," I said to myself aloud. I recalled reading that.

I looked at the puzzle again and whispered, "I'm going to finish this. Not to prove anything… but because I'm ready."

I placed another piece. Then my phone buzzed. A text from Maya.

My breath caught in surprise..

Maya: *We need to talk. Not tonight. Tomorrow, after church. Your place.*

Hope tackled me, I almost leaped out of my seat with joy. This was my shot and I would not mess it up.

I typed back only two words.

Me: *Thank you.*

With gratitude, I thought, wow…prayers really do work.

Armor Off

I woke before sunrise and sat at the edge of my bed, letting the early light stretch across the floor.

Today mattered.

Not because I needed to get her back.
Not because I feared losing her.

But because the man I had been for so long was no longer enough, and for the first time, I wasn't trying to outrun that truth.

I showered, shaved, and dressed without ceremony. A soft gray sweater. Black slacks. No suit. No armor. For years, I had learned how to look unbothered when I felt exposed. Today, I wanted to look like myself. Whatever that meant now.

I made coffee and let the fragrance of the rich dark roast fill the penthouse. I moved through each room slowly, straightening things, not to impress her, but to create space. Space for honesty. Space for a conversation I could not control but needed to enter with intention.

When I reached the puzzle room, I paused at the door.

I stepped inside and stood over the table, my eyes settling on the skyline I had begun rebuilding. Pieces were scattered across the surface. Some connected. Some turned the wrong way. None forced. None abandoned.

I picked up a piece and turned it between my fingers.

Not yet.

I set it back down and rested my hands on the table.

"God," I whispered, "be here today."

Downstairs, I placed a single white hydrangea in a small glass vase on the kitchen island. Maya's favorite. One flower. Not a bouquet. Not a grand gesture. Just something quiet. Something thoughtful. A whisper instead of a performance.

By late morning, my nerves began to hum, but they didn't take over. I checked the time. Walked to the window. Back to the kitchen. Up to the puzzle room. Then down again. Waiting, but not unraveling.

At 4:47 p.m., the elevator chimed.

I froze.

The knock followed seconds later, soft but deliberate.

I exhaled and opened the door.

Maya stood there calm and composed, beautifully herself. Her hair was pulled back. Her posture relaxed but guarded. Not cold. Just careful.

Bruno wasn't with her.

This wasn't casual.

"Hi Elijah," she said softly.

"Maya," I replied. "Come in."

She stepped inside, her eyes moving slowly through the space. She noticed the hydrangea immediately but didn't comment. She walked forward with care, as though the apartment itself required gentleness. As if truth might land hard if handled the wrong way.

I closed the door softly.

"Do you want water? Coffee? Tea?" I asked, careful not to fill the air with unnecessary noise.

"No," she said. "I just want to talk."

I nodded. "Okay."

We moved into the living room. She remained standing for a moment, arms loosely folded, not defensive, just grounding herself. I stayed where I was.

"I got your text," she said.

"I know."

"It felt different."

"How so?" I asked.

"It felt honest."

She held my gaze, searching. Then she nodded once.

"Elijah, I didn't pull away solely because of Emily."

I swallowed. She continued.

"I pulled away because I saw something in you that scared me," she said gently. "The silence. The shutting down. The way you folded into yourself instead of inviting me in. But the fact is, you let her in."

I lowered my eyes, not in shame, but in recognition.

"I've lived inside that silence before," she continued. "With my father, the greatest man I've known but after he died. I lived in the void of his absence and I watched my mother go through it. I realized I kept choosing the same absence because it's all I've known. But,

I've healed past that. I know what that path looks like and I'm not going back to that."

She paused, then steadied herself.

"I'm not angry at you for being human," she said. "But I need to feel your concern for me, too. I need someone I can trust fully…that matters to me. It's foundational."

I lifted my eyes, steady now.

"I'm listening," I said. "And you're right."

She looked at me differently now. Softer. Still discerning.

"I want to show you something," I said.

She hesitated, then nodded. "Okay."

I led her upstairs.

Open Doors

"You ready?" I asked softly.

"I'm here," she said. "Just open the door."

Her voice wasn't harsh.
It wasn't cold.

That made it heavier.

I inhaled once.
Twice.
Then I turned the knob.

The door opened.

Light spilled in first. Soft, natural light from the skylight above, like the room had been waiting all day for this moment. The air smelled faintly of paper and cardboard and years of quiet habits.

Maya stepped inside behind me.

And the room told on me before I ever could.

Puzzles everywhere, boxes…pieces. Half-finished. Abandoned. Some leaned against baseboards like old photographs no one had the heart to throw away. Shelves lined with boxes, labeled in my handwriting from years ago. A lifetime of beginnings that never quite became endings.

The largest table in the center held the newest one. Ours.

Missing only a few pieces.

She walked in slowly.

One step.
Then another.

She stopped.

Looked around.
And around again.

"Wow," she said quietly. "This is…"

I braced myself.

"A lot."

I swallowed. "Yeah."

She moved toward the table and touched one of the puzzle pieces lightly, her fingertips brushing the cardboard like she was afraid it might disappear if she pressed too hard.

"These are all yours?"

"Yes."

"Is this a collection?"

"Yes," I said. "…of past relationships…failed ones."

She nodded, taking that in with a deep, thoughtful breath.

"And this one?" she asked, gesturing to the skyline.

My throat tightened. "You."

She turned fully toward me then, really looking at me now, not just at the room.

"You've been doing this since you were a kid?"

I nodded. "My dad started it. My mom kept it going until she couldn't. After the divorce, the last puzzle was left unfinished. I walked in one day, and she'd thrown it away. She didn't know what it meant. She didn't understand that it mattered."

The words caught in my chest.

"And I stopped caring enough to try."

Maya held my gaze, breathing slow and steady.

"So these became the story of your relationships," she said quietly. "Every woman a puzzle."

"Yes and no," I said quickly. "More like… broken stories. Things I didn't know how to finish."

"And you kept all of them."

"Yes."

"But you didn't complete any of them."

My voice cracked before I could stop it.

"I couldn't."

She closed her eyes for a moment. When she opened them again, I saw it.

The hurt.
The compassion.
The understanding she didn't want to have.

"Elijah," she said softly, stepping closer. "Why did you bring me in here?"

"Because I care enough to finish this time."

Her expression softened, just for a second, like a door opening a few inches.

Then reality settled back into place.

"What happened while I was gone?" she asked gently.

"I told you."

"No," she said, shaking her head. "Not just her. You. What happened to *you*?"

I lowered my eyes.

She waited.

She always waited.

"After a few days of you gone," I whispered, "I panicked. I felt that old pull. The one that tells me everything good is temporary. And instead of fighting it, I let it make me quiet. I shut down. I shouldn't have. I know that."

She folded her arms loosely, not in defense, just grounding herself.

"I'm not judging you," she said. "I'm just trying to understand."

"I didn't do anything with Emily," I said quickly. "I didn't touch her. The moment she came inside, I wanted her out. Because of you. Because you're…"

I exhaled hard.

"You're the one I want."

She listened carefully, absorbing each word like she was deciding whether it could live inside her.

When I finished, she walked slowly around the room, studying the dozens of boxes, the scattered pieces, the broken almosts.

"Elijah," she said, tracing one of the frames lightly, "have you ever noticed something?"

"What?"

"You have all these puzzles. Pieces disconnected in every single one." She gestured around the room. "But the thing they all have in common?"

I waited.

"They're all parts of you," she said. "Memories you're holding onto. And healing isn't just finishing things. It's also choosing to let go of what no longer serves who you're becoming."

Her words hit the pit of my stomach.

She turned back to me, eyes softer than I deserved.

"You don't have to throw these away," she said quietly, gesturing around the room. "I'm not asking you to pretend your past didn't happen."

I didn't move. I barely breathed.

"But I need to know," she continued, "that you're not still living here. That you're not using these pieces as proof of who you've been instead of permission to become someone new."

I nodded slowly. My chest felt tight, but not panicked. Honest.

"That's why I tried something different." I said. "I went to church, Maya."

Her eyes widening, "You did?"

"Yes, I replied. "Not because I was trying to fix things between us. I just didn't know what to do next and I didn't want to hurt you or make my healing your burden."

She watched me carefully.

"I didn't know how to sit with myself anymore and there was no place to run," I went on. "I stayed after service. I listened. I prayed. I didn't even know how to do that.

Her expression didn't soften further. It steadied.

"They talked about surrender," I said. "About how God doesn't rush us, but He does ask us to stop hiding. I realized I've spent my whole life managing pain instead of healing it. I kept thinking if I understood it well enough, if I boxed it up neatly enough, it wouldn't hurt."

I gestured toward the puzzles.

"But all I did was preserve it."

Maya's eyes flicked back to the table, then to me.

"So what's different now?" she asked.

I stepped closer, not closing the space completely. Just enough to be present.

"I'm not trying to complete something to prove I can," I said. "I'm learning how to sit with what's unfinished without running. I'm learning how to ask God to help me stay."

I picked up one of the loose pieces from the table. Not the final one. Just one that fit somewhere I hadn't seen before.

"I don't know how long this takes," I said honestly. "I just know I'm not pretending anymore. And I'm not asking you to fill what only God can."

She exhaled slowly, like she'd been holding something in for days.

"That matters," she said.

We stood there in the quiet, the room no longer accusing, no longer heavy. Just truthful.

"I don't need you to be finished," she added. "I need you to be present."

I nodded. "I can do that."

She studied my face, searching for the old reflexes. The deflection. The retreat.

When she didn't find them, her shoulders lowered just a little.

"This doesn't mean everything is fixed," she said.

"I know."

"And it doesn't mean trust comes back all at once."

"I wouldn't expect it to."

She stepped closer then, close enough that I could feel her warmth, but she didn't touch me yet.

"It just means," she said softly, "that you finally invited me into the truth instead of the aftermath."

I swallowed hard. "That's all I've ever wanted to give you."

She reached out then, resting her hand lightly against my chest. Not claiming. Not promising. Just acknowledging.

"Then keep choosing that," she said. "Even when it scares you."

I covered her hand with mine, steady, intentional.

"I will."

And for the first time in that room, surrounded by all the pieces I hadn't known how to place, I didn't feel ashamed of what was unfinished.

I felt responsible for what came next.

Life Changed

The days that followed unfolded with a gentleness neither of us expected. There was no dramatic reconciliation, no emotional surge that burned bright only to collapse just as quickly. Instead, it felt like a slow inhale after holding your breath too long. Quiet. Intentional. Real.

Maya let herself be present again, but she didn't rush. I didn't push. We found a middle ground that felt earned, where honesty lived between us like a steady third pulse.

On Tuesday evening, she came over after work. She knocked lightly, an old habit, even though I'd told her more than once she never needed to knock again. I opened the door before her second tap.

She stepped inside with Bruno trotting proudly ahead of her, nails clicking against the marble like he owned the place. He inspected the living room thoroughly, sniffed the corners, then flopped onto the couch with a dramatic sigh, as if claiming it in the name of all dogs everywhere.

She shook her head. "He likes your apartment a little too much."

I smiled, kneeling to scratch behind his ears. "It's mutual."

Her lips curved, but her eyes lingered on me a second longer than usual. I could feel her noticing things. The way my shoulders weren't tense like they used to be. The absence of that restless edge I'd always carried. I wasn't withdrawn. I was settled.

"Did you eat?" I asked.

"I had a salad," she said. "But the salad offended me."

I laughed. "Offended?"

"Judgmental. Very leafy."

"Well," I said, stepping aside, "I made dinner."

She stopped. "You cooked?"

"I tried."

She raised an eyebrow. "Trying is honest."

In the kitchen, I'd laid out something simple. Roasted chicken. Vegetables. Rice. Nothing flashy. Nothing performative. Just warm food made with intention.

As we sat, I bowed my head.

Maya blinked. "You want to pray?"

"Yeah."

She reached for my hand without thinking. I took it, my thumb brushing lightly over her knuckles.

"God," I said quietly, "thank You for clarity. For patience. For another day. And for this woman. Amen."

She looked at me for a long moment afterward, something reverent softening her face.

"Elijah," she said quietly, "you're changing."

"I want to," I said.

We ate. We talked. About work. About Bruno. About the strange man who tried to hand her a pamphlet titled *Proper Sock Choices for Men.*

I laughed so hard I had to put my fork down.

Later, we moved to the couch. She tucked her legs beneath her. I angled toward her. Bruno wedged himself between us like an overeager mediator.

The television played quietly, forgotten.

"You seem grounded," she said.

"I feel grounded."

"What changed?"

I exhaled slowly. "That altar. I didn't go looking for anything. I just went because something pulled me. And I walked out feeling like the weight wasn't mine anymore."

She nodded. "Peace will do that."

"You helped me get there," I said.

She smiled softly. "I just cared enough to tell the truth."

Silence settled comfortably between us.

"What about the puzzles?" she asked.

"They're still becoming," I said. "Like me."

She studied me. "And the one on the table?"

"That one," I said, "is a story I don't want to abandon again. But only when we're ready."

She nodded slowly, something deep and thoughtful moving behind her expression.

After a moment, I stood and walked toward the kitchen.

"I want to give you something," I said when I returned.

I handed her a small envelope.

Her brow lifted as she opened it. Inside was a single key.

She looked up at me. "Elijah…"

"You don't have to knock anymore," I said quietly. "Come whenever you want. My home is open to you."

I hesitated, then added softly, "And so is my heart."

Her eyes filled before she could speak. She stood and stepped into me, wrapping her arms around me without hesitation.

I held her, one hand steady at the middle of her back, feeling the slow rise and fall of her breath against my chest.

When she pulled back, she didn't move far. Her hands remained at my sides, her fingers lightly gripping the fabric of my sweater. Her gaze lifted to mine, searching, vulnerable and certain at the same time.

"Elijah," she whispered, her voice barely there. "I don't know what to say."

"You don't have to say anything," I said.

For a moment, neither of us moved.

The space between us felt charged - full.

I leaned in slowly, giving her time to meet me if she wanted to.

She didn't hesitate.

Our lips met gently at first, almost cautious, the kind of kiss that asks a question before it makes a promise. But the moment she exhaled into it, the fire inside me grew.

Her hand tightened in my sweater.

I pulled her closer.

The second kiss came deeper, fuller, weeks of distance and restraint breaking open all at once. Not rushed. Not careless. Just heat and relief and recognition pouring through the space we had been holding between us.

She pressed closer, her body settling into mine like it belonged there. My hand moved to her waist, firm and steady, anchoring her as the kiss deepened, slower now, intentional, the kind that says, *I'm not going anywhere.*

When we finally broke apart, our foreheads rested together, both of us breathing heavier than before.

Her fingers were still curled into my sweater.

"Don't make me regret this," she whispered.

"I won't take you for granted again," I answered, softly. "Not ever."

This time when I kissed her, it was slower. Deeper. Not searching anymore.

And in that moment, the knowing settled in without question, without fear.

This was my woman.

Bruno lifted his head, watched us for a moment with mild disapproval, then dropped it back onto the cushion.

She let out a soft laugh against my shoulder.

And for the first time since everything between us had been tested, the future didn't feel fragile.

It felt real.

The Sweetest Thing

The rest of the week unfolded like a slow sunrise, warmth creeping in a little more each day, light reaching corners that had stayed dark for too long.

We didn't make love that night.

We held each other. We kissed. We stayed close. But there was no rush to cross that line. No urgency to prove anything with our bodies. For the first time, intimacy wasn't about passion alone. It was about trust learning how to breathe again.

I woke earlier than usual. Not from urgency, but from peace. I prayed longer, not searching for words, just sitting in the quiet and letting God sit with me. I moved through the world differently. Not perfect. Not polished. Not performing some new version of myself. Just grounded. Present. Awake.

Maya noticed immediately.

I didn't announce my growth. I lived it.
I didn't preach change. I practiced it.

I called her most mornings.
"Good morning. How'd you sleep?"

I texted her during the day, not constantly, not anxiously, but consistently. When we talked, I asked thoughtful questions about her day and listened, really listened, without preparing my response while she spoke. And when the day got heavy, when old instincts whispered to retreat, I stayed.

I didn't disappear.
Not once.

By Thursday evening, something between us felt steadier than it ever had before. That night, Maya invited me to her place for dinner. It was the first time since everything cracked open that she initiated time together.

When I arrived, she was barefoot in soft jeans that hug the curves of her small frame and a cream sweater, her hair down, her face fresh and unguarded. There was a quiet glow about her, not performative, not intentional, just present.

Bruno ran to me immediately, tail wagging like he'd been counting the minutes.

"You two are codependent," Maya teased as she closed the door behind me.

"Jealous?" I asked.

"Yes," Bruno barked.

She laughed, shaking her head. "Exactly."

Dinner was simple, salmon, rice, steamed vegetables, but Maya seasoned it like it was an act of worship. I took one bite and froze.

"Maya," I said seriously, "I'm trying not to fall deeper, but you're making this difficult."

She raised an eyebrow. "Because of the salmon?"

"Yes," I nodded. "If I propose someday, it will be because of this meal."

She burst out laughing, a full, unrestrained laugh that filled the room and settled something inside me I didn't realize had been restless.

"Let's not put that on the salmon," she said, wiping her eyes.

After dinner, we moved to the couch. Bruno claimed the rug, belly up, demanding attention at random intervals. I reached down occasionally to rub his stomach, earning dramatic sighs of approval.

A movie played in the background, something romantic Maya chose but neither of us was truly watching. What mattered was the space between us, or rather, the lack of it. This wasn't the closeness we'd had before. This felt earned.

Halfway through, Maya muted the TV.

I turned toward her. "Everything okay?"

She nodded, but there was something thoughtful behind her eyes.

"This feels right," she said quietly.

I shifted so I was fully facing her. "It does. There's no place I'd rather be."

She tucked one leg beneath her, settling sideways. She didn't pull away. She let the moment rest.

After a while, she leaned her head against my shoulder.

"You know what's strange?" she asked.

"What?"

"I'm not afraid with you. Not anymore."

I wrapped my arm around her, pulling her closer. "Good."

She hesitated, then whispered, "And I think… I think you're becoming someone I could trust with the deepest parts of me."

At that moment I realized how connected her words were to my chest. I instantly felt something sacred moved through the room. Quiet. Unannounced. Real.

I leaned down and kissed her, slow and intentional. Not hungry. Not rushed. A kiss that said I'm here. She responded immediately, her hand curling into my shirt, her body leaning into mine like she belonged there.

"Maya," I said softly between kisses, "there's a cookout tomorrow."

She smiled faintly. "Thanks for cooling that off."

She paused, took in a deep breath like she was trying to focus, "That sounds fun."

I smiled, "I'd like you to come with me and meet my best friend. Marcus."

Her brows lifted slightly. "Best friend?"

"Yes," I admitted. "he's like family to me."

She studied my face, then nodded slowly. "Okay."

Relief washed through me.

We kissed again, more intensely this time. When we finally settled back, she shifted until she was lying against my chest, her head resting just below my collarbone. I wrapped both arms around her instinctively, holding her like my body had been built for this exact shape.

Her breathing slowed. Mine followed. Rhythm.

Nothing in my life had ever felt like this. Not success. Not control. Not achievement.

She was the sweetest thing I've ever experienced.

The weight of her trust, the certainty. The peace of not bracing for loss.

I stared at the ceiling, heart full and steady, and made a silent vow I didn't yet have language for.

Whatever this was, I would protect it.
Not with fear.
Not with control.
But with presence. With consistency. With the kind of love that rooted deeply.

I pressed my lips gently to her hair.

Tomorrow, she would meet Marcus.
Tomorrow, the world would see us together.

But tonight, she rested against my chest, and I knew I would never let this slip through my hands again.

A Calm Storm

Marcus had always believed food solved most things.

Not in a way he ever said out loud. You just knew it by the way he hosted. The table stayed full, the music stayed low, and the room somehow found its rhythm without anyone needing to name what they were feeling.

It was his way of loving people without asking them to explain themselves.

So when he texted earlier in the week, *Don't forget to pull up Saturday. Just vibes*, I didn't ask questions. I never did with Marcus. Minimal explanation. Maximum confidence. He trusted the moment to do the work.

We arrived together.

Maya stepped out of the car first, and I felt it before I even saw it happen. The shift. The recalibration. The way attention bent without being summoned.

She wore a deep green dress that didn't cling or shout or sparkle. It simply existed, like it knew it didn't need permission. It framed her without trying to shape her. Her hair fell loose over her shoulders, and there was something about the way she moved that made the night feel quieter, like the room itself leaned in.

People noticed. Not because she demanded it. Because she didn't.

Marcus opened the door with his usual grin and pulled me into a bear hug, clapping my shoulder hard enough to rattle my chest.

"There he is," he said, pulling back and scanning me. "Man looks lighter. What did you do, switch vitamins or something?"

I smirked. "Something like that."

He turned to Maya, eyes lighting up immediately. "And you must be the reason he stopped ghosting life."

Maya smiled, calm and unbothered. "I can't take credit for good vitamins."

Marcus laughed loud and genuine. "I like her already."

The apartment buzzed the way good nights do. Music humming under conversation. Glasses clinking. People drifting in and out of loose circles, laughter rising and falling naturally. It felt good. Familiar. Like a version of life I hadn't realized I'd been holding my breath away from.

And then the door opened again.

Emily walked in like she had rehearsed the moment.

She paused just long enough for the room to register her presence. Not awkward. Strategic. Hair flawless. Outfit deliberate. Confidence worn like armor polished daily. Her eyes swept the space quickly, efficiently, and landed on me.

Then they landed on Maya.

Something flickered. Gone as fast as it came.

Marcus turned, surprised. "Oh. You made it."

Emily smiled brightly. "Of course. I was already in the area."

She moved closer, placing herself just inside the circle, close enough to be included but not invited. Her gaze never fully left me, even when she spoke to others. Maya noticed. She always noticed.

Maya didn't shift. Didn't tense. She simply watched.

As conversation resumed, Emily began to weave herself in, thread by thread. Small comments. Casual callbacks. References designed to sound effortless but land precisely where they were meant to.

"Remember that place downtown," Emily said lightly, eyes on me. "The one with the ridiculous cocktails?"

I nodded, polite. "Yeah."

Maya tilted her head just slightly. "Oh?"

Emily smiled. "We used to go there sometimes."

The air changed. Subtle. Immediate.

Marcus frowned. "Wait. You two knew each other?"

The question landed clean and loud, like a glass set down too hard.

Emily hesitated. Just long enough to matter.

"Yes," she said. "We've known each other for a while."

Maya smiled politely, her tone calm. "That's interesting. Elijah never mentioned you."

Emily gave a quick laugh. "Some things don't always come up."

Maya's voice stayed warm. "I imagine that's true. I've found that when something matters, it usually does."

"Well, not all things known need to be spoken of." Emily curtly said, gazing toward me.

The room went still.

“Baby, we can go.” I said quickly, eyes firmly on Maya.

She didn’t move.

Then she spoke, her tone gracious and steady.

“No, we don’t have to.”

She looked at Emily.

“I hope you don’t mind me saying this, but it feels like you’re trying to prove something tonight.”

Emily blinked. “I don’t know what you mean.”

Maya met her eyes fully now. No flinch. No apology.

“I think you do.”

Silence stretched, thick and undeniable.

“This isn’t a competition,” Maya said gently. “And if it were, I wouldn’t want to win it like this.”

Emily flushed. “You don’t know anything about me.”

Maya nodded. “That’s true. But I know what desperation looks like when it dresses itself up as confidence.”

The words were quiet.

They landed anyway.

Emily glanced around the room, aware now of every set of eyes. She grabbed her purse and moved towards the door.

“I didn’t come here to be humiliated.”

Marcus opened his mouth to speak, then stopped.

Maya spoke one last time. “I hope you find peace. Truly.”

Emily left.

The door shut behind her with a sound that felt permanent.

Marcus exhaled slowly. “Damn.”

He turned to me. “For the record bro, I had no idea you two had history. She hit me up on social media. Seemed cool. Nice looking. Persistent. I figured, why not.”

I chuckled. “Can’t blame you.

I shook my head. “It’s old. And it’s done.”

He studied me for a long moment. “You good?”

I looked at Maya, standing steady beside me, unshaken.

“Better than I’ve been in a long time.”

Then he looked at Maya, “Are you good?”

“Of course.” Smiled and looked at me.

Throwing up his hands, Marcus shouted, “One monkey don’t stop no show. Where’s my game.”

“Here we go.” I said and he grabbed the box and shouted, “Scrabble.”

“Oh yea, let’s play.” Maya was ready.

Marcus was a beast but he met his match that night.

Maya annihilated everyone.

Marcus stared at the board like it had personally betrayed him. "This feels personal."

"Words matter," Maya said calmly, placing another devastating tile. "Boom."

Everyone cheered, high-fived me like I was responsible for the scrabble storm that just passed through to finally shut the king of trash talk down.

I stepped behind her, resting a kiss into her hair. She leaned back into me without thinking, smiling.

The night rolled on as if nothing had happened.

And somehow, everything had changed.

I knew it then, with a clarity that settled deep and quiet in my chest.

Whatever I had been chasing before, whatever ghosts I had mistaken for connection, whatever noise I once thought was passion, none of it compared to this.

This woman.
This steadiness.
This peace.

And I understood one thing I had never understood before.

Love.

It wasn't loud, it couldn't be forced and I had finally found it.

New Levels

The walk to her place slowed me down in ways I didn't expect.

Not because I was tired, I was strangely hyper-aware.

In a way that felt almost entirely physical. I could hear the sound of her breathing, variance in her voice, and the cadence of our steps syncing without effort. I could feel the night air brushing my skin, cool and clean, like it was trying to steady something already moving too fast inside me.

Her hand brushed mine once.

Brief. Innocent.

Then it happened again.

This time, she must've felt the spark charging through me because she quickly pulled away. As if she were reminding herself not to make sudden moves.

Even her restraint did something to me.

At her door, she paused with the key halfway in the lock. The hallway light caught the curve of her jaw, the calm in her posture. She didn't rush. She never rushed. That was part of her gravity.

"You want a nightcap?" she asked, light, almost casual, like she wasn't fully aware of the undercurrent humming between us.

I met her eyes. Held them. Let the moment breathe.

"Yeah, sure." Trying to appear composed.

I was completely intoxicated with her.

Inside, her place wrapped around me immediately. It felt like her. Soft lighting that didn't try to impress. Clean lines without sterility. A quiet hum beneath everything, the kind that told you someone actually lived here. Not staged. Not transitional. I felt like a home.

"I'm going to shower," she said, setting her bag down. "Make yourself comfortable."

The door closed behind her, and a moment later the water started.

I sat on the couch, elbows on my knees, hands loosely clasped. My jaw tightened without my permission. My body was already responding, anticipation stirring low and undeniable, heat waking up in a way that didn't ask for approval with just the thought of her undressing to shower.

I breathed through it.

"Stop. It's not time." I said repeatedly to myself.

This wasn't about denying desire. It was about knowing what to do with it.

When she came back into the room, I forgot how to breathe for a second.

The pajamas were ridiculous and perfect all at once. Soft fabric that skimmed her body, playful without trying, fitted just enough to make imagination dangerous. Her hair was pulled back, skin still warm from the shower, face bare and open in a way that felt more intimate than anything she could have put on.

She caught the look in my eyes and smiled slightly. Not coy but knowingly.

"What?" she asked.

I shook my head once. "Nothing. Everything."

She laughed softly and sat beside me.

Too close.

Her thigh brushed mine. Once. Then again. Her hand came to rest against my arm, fingers warm, grounding and tempting at the same time. The movie she put on faded almost immediately into background noise, the sound reduced to texture rather than story.

When she leaned in, I met it without hesitation.

The kiss started slow. Exploratory. A meeting, of passion. My hand found her waist naturally, fitting there like it had always known the shape. Her fingers slid into my jacket, curling at my back, pulling me closer with quiet certainty.

Not asking.

Inviting.

She leaned in fully now, and her breath caught softly against my mouth. That sound alone nearly undid me. Something sharp and urgent surged through my body, desire rising fast, demanding release, demanding permission.

My body answered fully. There was no denying it. Heat. Pressure. Want.

And she felt every inch.

She didn't pull away.

She pressed closer.

Her body followed mine, trusting, present, wanting. The closeness tipped something inside me from longing into danger. Not because she stopped me.

But because she didn't.

That was the moment restraint mattered most.

I broke the kiss, lifted myself off her, breath uneven, forehead resting against hers as I fought the roar in my chest.

My hands stayed where they were, anchoring instead of retreating, choosing presence over impulse.

"It's not time," I said quietly.

Those words cost me.

She stayed close, eyes searching my face, breathing just as unsteady. Desire still lived there, alive and waiting, but so did understanding.

She nodded once.

Not in rejection.

In agreement.

I lifted my head and looked to the ceiling for a moment, grounding myself and said, "You really have changed me."

The truth of it settled between us, heavy and real.

I looked back at her, voice low, steady, unguarded. "Maya… I love you."

She didn't hesitate.

Her hands came up to my jaw, holding my face with intention, with certainty. "Elijah," she said softly, "I love you too."

We stayed there like that for a while. Bodies close. Heat unresolved. No pretending it wasn't there. No urgency to extinguish it either.

This wasn't denial.

It was stewardship.

And for the first time in my life, restraint didn't feel like loss.

It felt like strength.

"I'm going to go." I said, before I went too far.

She walked me to the door a few minutes later. No awkwardness. No regret. Just warmth and promise held carefully between us.

When I stepped outside her apartment, I turned once more.

"Goodnight," I said.

"Goodnight," she replied.

And as the door closed gently behind me, I walked slowly to my car - chest full, body calm, spirit settled.

Nothing in my life had ever felt like that.

And I knew, with a quiet surety, that I would spend the rest of my life protecting what this had become.

I didn't sleep much that night.

Not because of regret but because I knew what to do next.

Morning After

Desire still moved through my body, a low, steady reminder of how close I had come, how easily I could have crossed a line that once would not have stopped me.

Yet this time, desire didn't feel the way it used to, like something that needed to be satisfied or silenced. This was different. It felt contained. Honored. Like strength I was finally learning how to hold without letting it take the wheel.

I lay awake staring at the ceiling long after the apartment had gone still, long after the city sounds thinned into a distant hum. The darkness felt intentional, almost sacred. I replayed the moment I stopped. Not with pride. Not with regret.

With clarity.

I hadn't stopped because I was afraid of wanting her. God knew I wanted her. I had never wanted anyone like this. I stopped because I wanted to do it right.

Not just chemistry.
Not just another passionate moment, that was easy

I had lived there before, in the intoxicating rush of connection without foundation. Inside of the aftermath of bad choices, surveying the wreckage once my adrenaline faded and the feelings changed.

I didn't want that life anymore.

I wanted to be her husband.
I wanted God's approval.
I wanted a family that didn't feel like a question mark.

Maya had told me once, almost in passing, about her father. She didn't dramatize it or collapse into grief when she spoke. She simply stated it, the way people do when they've carried something heavy for so long it's become part of their posture. He died when she was eleven. One moment present. The next gone.

That kind of loss doesn't shout. It settles. It shapes the way you love, the way you wait, the way you trust. It teaches you that the people you need most can disappear without warning.

Lying there in the dark, I understood something with sudden, piercing precision.

If I crossed that line too soon, if I let desire outrun devotion, I wouldn't just be risking a moment. I would be risking trust. And for Maya, trust had already been taken once without explanation.

I wasn't going to be another man who stayed physically present while disappearing emotionally. And I wasn't going to give bad choices even the slightest opportunity to fracture what God was clearly building between us.

By morning, the decision had settled into me with weight and certainty.

I didn't debate it.
I didn't delay.

I called the pastor before fear or logic could interfere.

"Can I come see you today?" I asked.

There was a pause on the other end, then a calm, almost knowing reply.
"I was hoping you would."

The church office was quiet when I arrived. Sunlight streamed through tall windows, catching dust motes that floated lazily in the stillness. The building didn't feel grand or imposing. It felt grounded. Like it wasn't trying to impress anyone. Like it was simply making space.

The pastor greeted me warmly and gestured toward a chair.

"Sit," he said. "Tell me what's on your mind."

I leaned forward, hands loosely clasped. I didn't feel guarded. I didn't feel the need to perform. My posture was open. My eyes steady.

"I want to marry Maya and do this right," I said. "Her father isn't here for me to ask for her hand. So I'm asking you."

He didn't interrupt. He didn't rush me. He just listened, the way men do when they're taking you seriously.

"And what does doing it right look like to you?" he asked.

I stared at the floor for a moment.

Images surfaced uninvited. My father's back as he walked away. My mother's quiet strength as she learned how to carry everything alone. Years spent mastering control, ambition, solitude. Relationships entered confidently and exited cleanly, before they ever demanded vulnerability or permanence.

"It looks like staying in every way," I said finally. "Even when I don't know how. Even when every instinct in me tells me to pull back."

The pastor studied me carefully.

"And what does it mean to you to be a husband?"

I inhaled deeply, feeling the weight of the word settle in my chest.

"It means loving her even when it's hard," I said. "Not perfection. Not control but showing up emotionally, physically, peacefully. Choosing her every day. Learning how to enjoy her, not manage her. Protecting her heart in ways I didn't know how to protect my own."

He leaned back slightly, letting the words breathe.

"There's something you should know," he said gently. "Maya lost her father young. Tragic accident. No warning. She's carried that longer than she lets on."

"Yes sir," I said. "She told me."

I paused, then added quietly, "That's why I want to do right by her."

His eyes softened.

"I don't care how uncomfortable this makes me," I continued. "I don't care how exposed I feel. I won't leave her holding unanswered questions. I won't be another absence she has to make sense of."

He stood and placed a hand on my shoulder.

"Son," he said, "you're not speaking from fear. You're speaking from love and understanding."

Then he smiled, warm and assured.

"If Maya would have you," he said, "I would be honored to marry you both."

I exhaled a breath I hadn't realized I'd been holding.

"Thank you," I said quietly.

That afternoon, I went to the jeweler and chose a custom four-carat princess-cut diamond set in 14-karat gold. It was elegant, timeless, and quite striking. The kind of piece that didn't try to impress but was simply impressive.

I stood there for a long moment before purchasing it, hoping she would see in it what I did.

When I left, I drove home with a calm I had never known before. Not excitement, not anxiety.

Purpose.

I went straight to the puzzle room.

The unfinished puzzle waited on the table, pieces scattered in familiar disarray. I sat down, rolled up my sleeves, and began sorting deliberately. No rushing. No forcing pieces into places they didn't belong.

Piece by piece, the image revealed itself.

When only one piece remained, I stopped.

I didn't place it.

Instead, I picked up my phone and sent a single message.

Me: *Will you be at church tomorrow?*

The reply came minutes later.

Maya: *Yes.*

I smiled.

Before doubt could enter, I called Marcus.

He answered on the second ring. "This better be good."

"I'm proposing," I said.

Silence. Then laughter. "You lying?!"

"Nope," I said. "Tomorrow. At church, got the ring and everything."

Another pause. Longer this time. "You got a ring! Bro, no way."

"It's happening."

Then, he shouted. "It's about dang time! Congratulations, man. Just so you know, I'm starting the bachelor party planning tonight."

I laughed. "She still has to say yes."

"If she's smart, she'll run."

"Now, that's cold," I said. "You know she's smart. Do I need to bring her back for another game of…"

"Don't you finish that sentence." he laughed. "Hey, I went easy."

"Sure you did. I'll see you tomorrow."

When I ended the call, I texted the address and sat for a moment taking it in.

This was it.

Tomorrow was the day and I was ready for it.

The Final Piece

I arrived at the church earlier than necessary.
Hours earlier.

I sat in my car longer than I planned to, my hands resting on the steering wheel as I watched people move through the front doors in small, ordinary groups. Families holding hands. Couples leaning into each other. Individuals walking alone, shoulders carrying things no one else could see.

I had been one of them once.
In many ways, I still was.

But today was different.
Today was intentional.

When I finally stepped inside, the sanctuary met me with the quiet dignity of polished wood and the faint scent of perfume lingering in the air. The worship team rehearsed softly, familiar hymns floating through the room like something remembered instead of performed.

I took a seat near the back. The framed puzzle rested beside me, carefully wrapped, leaning against my leg like a promise I hadn't spoken aloud yet.

As the service began, I listened differently than I ever had before.

Not defensively.
Not skeptically.
Open.

The message wasn't dramatic. No theatrics. No emotional manipulation. Just truth spoken plainly about love, about change, about how holding everything together can sometimes be the very thing that keeps you from becoming whole.

The song that followed was one I'd heard before, but today it landed differently.

I surrender to You, Lord.

A few rows behind me, the doors creaked open. Marcus slipped inside, scanning the room like a man who had clearly been searching for fulfillment in the wrong places. His eyes followed the women walking past, his brows lifting appreciatively.

He leaned down, whispering just loud enough for me to hear.

"Bro… I've been hanging out at the wrong spots. Why you ain't invite me here sooner?"

I didn't turn my head.
"Chill."

Marcus grinned. "I'm just saying. Church got options."

"God first," I murmured. "The rest will come."

He chuckled softly. "Relax, man. I'm messing with you. This is the day." His tone shifted, sincerity cutting through the humor. "I'm happy for you. She's perfect for you."

I swallowed. "She hasn't said yes yet."

Marcus leaned back, eyes forward. "Well then," he said quietly, "let's see what happens."

As the service neared its closing, the pastor returned to the pulpit, a knowing smile on his face.

"Before we dismiss," he said, "we have something special today."

My heart began to pound.

I stood, picked up the wrapped frame, and carried it forward carefully, reverently, as if it held more than glass and wood.

Maya sat halfway up the sanctuary. She had come in late, slipping quietly into a seat, unaware of what was about to happen. When she saw me walking toward the front, her brow furrowed in confusion.

The pastor handed me the microphone as I turned to face the congregation.

"I spent most of my life believing that if I could just keep everything together, I'd be okay," I began. "I learned how to succeed. How to lead. How to stand strong."

I let the words settle before finishing.

"But I never learned how to stay."

The room grew silent.

"I convinced myself that love was for other people," I continued. "That it was something I didn't need… or maybe something I wouldn't ever have."

I exhaled slowly, the truth of it sitting heavier now that it had been said out loud.

"So I built a life that didn't make room for it."

Then I turned toward her.

"Maya," I said, softer this time, "finding you didn't just change how I see love…"

I paused, letting my eyes hold hers.

"It showed me what was really missing in my life…God."

I stepped closer, the framed puzzle steady in my hands, every piece finally where it was supposed to be.

Then I held it out to her.

She took it slowly, pulling back the wrapping. As her eyes moved over the image, recognition settled in. The skyline. The story. Us.

Before she could look up, I lowered myself to one knee.

"He who finds a wife finds a good thing," I said, my voice steady even as emotion pressed against my chest.

Her eyes widened, shock and understanding rising at the same time.

"And you, Maya… are a good thing."

I reached into my jacket, pulled out the ring, and opened the box.

"Will you marry me?"

For a moment, the world went completely still.

Then Maya stood, tears already falling as she stepped toward me. She set the frame gently aside, knelt in front of me, and cradled my face in her hands.

"Yes," she said through laughter and tears. "Yes."

The sanctuary erupted.

Behind me, Marcus let out a long whistle and started clapping. "That's my guy."

I stood and pulled Maya into my arms, holding her not like someone afraid to lose her, but like a man whose missing pieces had finally fallen into place.

Epilogue

The room no longer held puzzles.

It held two cribs.

I stood in the doorway with Maya tucked into my side, her body fitting into mine the way breath fits into lungs. Not something you notice until it's missing.

One of my arms rested around her shoulders, the other firm at her back, not out of fear, not out of vigilance, but out of instinct. The kind that no longer asks permission.

The twins slept side by side, their small chests rising and falling in quiet synchronization, as if they had agreed on the rhythm long before they entered the world. Even in sleep, they moved together. Even now, they understood something about connection.

Above their cribs hung the framed puzzle.

Complete.

The soft glow of the nightlight touched the glass, the pieces aligned so seamlessly that you couldn't tell where one ended and another began. What once felt impossible now felt inevitable.

Our daughter, ***Jael Ruth***, slept with her tiny fist curled near her cheek, her brow faintly furrowed, determined even in rest.

Ruth, named of my mother.

The woman who taught me strength without ever naming it. The woman who stayed although it was hard and unnoticed and heavy. The woman who carried love like a treasure instead of performance.

I could already see her in Jael.

Quiet strength. Steady will. A spirit that would not bend easily.

Beside her, **Joel Samuel** shifted softly, a small sound escaping his lips that almost sounded like a laugh.

Samuel, named after Maya's father.

Gone too soon, but never absent from the way she loves. From the way she shows up. From the way she holds people without needing recognition.

Maya leaned into me without speaking, her head settling against my chest like it had always belonged there.

"They were restless earlier," she whispered. "Aunt Toni rocked them forever."

I smiled, the sound silent but full. "She's good at that."

As if summoned by the mention of her name, Aunt Toni appeared quietly in the doorway behind us. She had come to help because neither of our mothers were here to do it.

She had arrived when Maya went in labor, without ceremony, suitcase in hand, sleeves already rolled up, love already activated.

She looked at the twins, then at us, her eyes soft with something reverent.

"Come here," she said gently.

We gathered instinctively. Maya reached for my hand. I tightened my grip.

Aunt Toni placed one hand on each of our shoulders, then bowed her head.

"Father God," she began, her voice low and steady, the kind of voice that had learned how to speak to heaven without hesitation. "Thank You for this family. Thank You for these children. Thank You for the love You built here, piece by piece."

Something warm pressed behind my eyes.

"Cover them," she continued. "When they're tired. When they're unsure. When life stretches them in ways they didn't expect. Give them wisdom where they feel confusion. Patience where they feel pressure. And a peace that does not depend on circumstances."

Maya's fingers tightened in mine.

"Bless these babies," Aunt Toni whispered. "Let them grow up surrounded by safety. By truth and consistency. Let them always know they are wanted. Let them always know they are loved. And let them never question that You are near."

She paused, her voice softening.

"And thank You for the mothers who aren't here… but whose love is still living through them."

"In Jesus' name, Amen," we said together.

Silence followed - holy and full.

When she lifted her head, her eyes shone. She kissed Maya's cheek, then mine.

"I'm heading to bed," she said. "I leave early in the morning."

I nodded, my throat tight. "Thank you. For everything."

She smiled. "This is what family does, baby."

When she disappeared down the hall, Maya and I stood there a little longer, listening to the quiet rhythm of the nursery.

"This feels surreal," she whispered.

I kissed the top of her head. "It's real babe. Us."

Later, when we climbed into bed, the house breathing with new life around us, I lay staring at the ceiling, thinking about all the roads that had led here.

I didn't have a single regret.

"Elijah," Maya called my gently as if she read my thoughts.

"I'm here," I answered.

"I love you." She said softly.

She turned toward me, the faint moonlight slipping through the window, catching her smile just enough to make it glow in the dark.

"I love you too."

I leaned in brushing my lips against hers before pulling her close, feeling the softness of her silk pajamas and warm skin in my hands.

"You are God's greatest gift to me," I said.

She let out a quiet laugh. "What about the babies?"

I smiled at her. "There are no babies without you. Now, let's work on set number two."

She shifted slightly, giving me a look even in the dim light. "You can't be serious. Do you realize what I just endured." She playfully pulled away.

I laughed under my breath. "Relax. I'm joking. Come here."

This time I pulled her closer, settling her against my chest, feeling her soften into me without resistance.

“Goodnight, babe,” she said, her voice already quieter.

“Goodnight.”

And in that quiet, everything finally fit.

Dear Reader

If you've made it here, thank you - not just for reading, but for allowing yourself to feel.

Missing Pieces was written for the quiet spaces we learn to live in… the ones we don't always have the language for.

If you saw yourself in Elijah or either character, even for a moment, then you understand:

You can be successful and still feel empty.
You can be strong and still be wounded.
You can love… and still not know how to receive it.

But here's the truth, what's missing in your life is not always a person.

Sometimes… it's God.

Only God can heal what we've hidden and restore what we've lost.

Not religion. Not routine. But relationship with the Most High.

You are not too far gone, too broken, or too guarded for Him.

Wholeness is not something you build. It's something you surrender into.

If this stirred something in you… don't ignore it.

Lean into it.

God wants to give you more than you could ever measure.

Reese

STAY CONNECTED

Instagram: @authreese
TikTok: @auth.reese
Website: www.reesewordlaw.com

www.amazon.com/author/reesewordlaw

www.ingramcontent.com/pod-product-compliance
Lightning Source LLC
LaVergne TN
LVHW090600110826
845146LV00001B/204

* 9 7 9 8 9 8 8 4 1 2 0 3 8 *